Published by Autumn Day Publishing
Copyright 2015
Other works by L.S. Gagnon,
Witch: A New Beginning
Witch: The Spell Within
Witch: The Secret of the Leaves
Witch: The Final Chapter
Thea: The Little Witch, Into the Forest
ISBN 978-0-9967707-0-5
All characters in this book are fiction
and figments of the author's imagination.
If you want to receive our monthly newsletter, text the
word 'witch' to 42828 to sign up.

Thea: The Little Witch

The Power of Believing

By L.S. Gagnon

A special thanks to Shelby Arruda, Miranda Palafox, and Abigail Nelson. Thank you for being my little witches. And to Zachary and Aidan Halliwell, thank you for all you do. It means the world to me.

I would also like to dedicate this book to my precious Salem. I will never grow tired of you. I will always find magic and inspiration when I visit. I hope to one day call you my home.

TABLE OF CONTENTS

Prologue

Seasons come and go, but friends can stay in our hearts forever. We can think of them when we close our eyes, remember them in our dreams. But most of all, we can never forget how much we loved them.

My life as a child was changing; humans were now a part of who I was. I had come to love them, come to need them. I never imagined that one day I would have to lose them.

Chapter One: Punished

I stayed very quiet as my wizard father sat at the kitchen table and read his book. He would glance at me from time to time before looking back at the pages. It was my seventh week being kept in my little corner of the cottage. I kept tapping my foot, waiting for my jail time to end.

I had to spend a whole hour, every day, in the same spot, until my father was done reading. When my hour was done, I was not allowed to stay out for very long. In fact, when I was outside, I had a long list of chores I had to get done. I wasn't complaining; I was lucky to even be breathing right now.

Sharron, a witch that lived next door, had told my father that humans had seen me flying over the forest—a rule a little witch like me was not supposed to break. Although it was true I had done that, I also had a very good reason.

My new friends and I had been lost while begging for treats, and flying over the forest was the only way to see where we were. I didn't even know humans had seen us. I actually thought I had gotten away with it, until Sharron ratted me out, that is.

She was quick to inform my father that humans were in an uproar over what they had seen—or thought they did. My father was furious with me. It had taken him all that night to go from village to village and erase human memories.

That was the kind of wizard magic my father had. Powerful magic others could only dream of, others but me, of course.

I was proud to be half wizard, and even prouder to also be half witch. With my larger build than most little witches, I was proud to be who I was. Although my father didn't like it when I used my magic, I never let that stop me. I had even used my magic in front of my new *human* friends— which is why I was punished right now.

Misunderstandings lead me to reveal many secrets to them. They thought I was trick or treating, and *I* thought they knew I was a real witch. I feared my father would erase me from their memories, but to my surprise, he let them remember that whole day. They gave their word about never revealing the fact that witches were real. They had no problem with me being a real witch. In fact, they thought it was the most thrilling news.

Zachary and Miri, two of the humans, had already been to my house twice. I made a sour face when my father had quickly sent them on their way. *"Thea is grounded,"* he'd said.

Aidan, their brother, was still not allowed on his feet. He was a boy whose foot I had *fixed* when I thought they knew I was a real witch. My father had to *unfix* him for a while so his parents wouldn't realize I had used magic on him. My father had put a false memory into Aidan's parents' heads. Now they thought Aidan had taken a bad fall, and that his foot was getting better because of that.

Cory, one of my best friends, and a witch, had become very good friends with Zachary, the oldest of the humans. Cory loved to show Zachary all the spells he knew. I'd sit by the window and watch them—wishing I could be out there with them.

But today was my last day of jail. Once my hour was up, I would be allowed to play with my friends again. Delia, my other best friend, also a witch, couldn't wait to tell me what I had missed.

"They're doing it again," she said the other day while talking to me through the window.

She was talking about the humans, and how they were cutting down trees again. They would put pretty things all over them and display them by their window. It happened every year around this time, and I was determined to find out why.

I looked at my father again, hoping my hour was almost up. The hourglass, which sat in front of him, hadn't moved in what seemed like hours. There was still plenty of sand making its way to the other side.

I sighed and tapped my foot faster. The morning had quickly passed, and I didn't want to miss the afternoon. I didn't blame my father for being so harsh on me. Truth was, I was surprised he only grounded me for seven weeks.

Again, I sighed.

"One hour," my father said, turning another page. He didn't even look at me. He kept his sparkling green eyes on his book.

I bit my lip, hoping my witch mother would grant me an early release. She had tried to plead my case, but my father wouldn't have it.

"Emma, she flew over the forest, and was seen by humans," he reminded her.

My mother was usually able to soften my father's heart, but not this time.

"He has a point, Thea," she had told me.

I knew I'd lost when she said that.

But I had taken my punishment like a champ. As my father read his book, I had sighed, tapped my foot, bit my nails, counted the spots on the wall, and drove him crazy. I knew he was as happy as I was that my jail time was nearly over.

I looked at the hourglass again, it still looked pretty full.

"Did you turn the hourglass over?" I asked.

My father slowly looked my way. "No, but I can," he said, giving me that look people give when they're looking over their glasses.

I bit my lip and started counting the spots on the wall again. This was the longest hour on earth. I let out another long, anguished sigh. My heart sank when my father reached for the hourglass.

"Sigh again," he said with his hand on the hourglass. "We could go for two hours, if you wish."

I put my head down. "I'll be quiet, Father."

"You don't have to be quiet," he said, pulling his hand away from the hourglass. "I just need you to understand what you did wrong."

He closed his book and rose to his feet. I still had my head down when he stood in front of me. "Look at me, Thea."

I slowly looked up at him. His wavy brown hair was a bit of a mess right now. He'd been running his fingers through his hair a lot lately, especially when I was in trouble.

"You know why I was so harsh this time, don't you?" he asked.

"Yes, Father."

"And why is that?"

"Um, because humans saw me flying?"

He let out a long sigh, seeming frustrated, and squatted down. "Thea, I was harsh because you put our world in danger. Humans don't understand witches, much less a wizard. And when people don't understand something, they can be cruel. I would die if anyone ever hurt you," he said, brushing his fingers along my face. "You and your mother are my world, my loves. There isn't anything I wouldn't do for you. But there is one thing you must understand, you are a very special nine year old little girl, and some humans may see you as a danger to them. Can you understand that?"

I looked into his eyes, trying to understand.

"I would never hurt anyone," I answered.

He nodded knowingly. "Of course you wouldn't. But humans don't know you, do they? They don't even know witches are real. Imagine what they would do if they ever found out about wizards. That would put our world in danger, Thea."

I was starting to see his point. I thought back to the men who had pointed their pitch forks at me and my friends. They wanted to hurt us that day. They had seen us flying, and had quickly gathered together to throw us in jail for being witches. I was starting to realize how stupid I had been. I would never want to put my family and friends in danger.

"I think I understand, Father."

He looked into my eyes, after a few moments, he smiled. "Yes, I believe you do, Thea."

I knew my father was reading my mind. It was something wizards knew how to do. Although my ability to read minds hadn't developed yet, my father had no doubt that I would mature that wizard part of me as I got older.

My mother walked in as my father was still talking to me. His green eyes lit up when he looked at her. "And there is the other love of my life," my father said, as he rose to his feet.

My mother, a witch, gave him a warm smile. My father stroked her long, brown hair. "Are they still waiting?" my father asked.

My mother smiled. "Yes, both of them, and they've been out there all morning."

I quickly looked out the window. I knew my mother was referring to Cory and Delia, my best friends.

My father chuckled softly. "I suppose it's been about an hour, don't you?" he said, pulling my mother into his arms.

She ran her fingers along his cheek. "I think she's learned her lesson. I don't think she'll be flying around any time soon."

"Not a chance," I quickly said.

My heart was racing. Was he about to release me from my jail time?

"It would be a shame to keep her friends waiting," my father said.

"Oh, they *hate* waiting," I quickly informed him.

I could see my father's shoulders bouncing up and down as he laughed quietly.

"Did you hear that, William? They *hate* waiting," my mother said, raising one eyebrow.

He nodded, pulled away from her, and turned to face me. "Okay, Thea. Your hour is up. You may go play with your friends now."

I quickly jumped to my feet before he could change his mind. "One moment," my father said before I could head for the door.

I froze.

"Yes, Father?"

He clamped his hands behind his back and glared down at me. "I have some rules for you, young lady."

I looked at my mother, but she pointed to my father. "Your father is speaking to you."

I was doomed. I was hoping my sad eyes would make my mother jump in to help me. Luck was not on my side. I faced my father and prepared myself for the rules I knew I was going to hate.

"No magic," he began. "No spells, no flying, no going too far, and no waving your hand. Do you understand?"

He just took the fun out of my day.

"Yes, Father," I said, putting my head down.

"One more thing," he said, lifting my chin. "No casting spells on humans."

Okay, now my day was going to be boring.

"Yes, Father."

"Now run along," my mother said. "I want you back here for dinner."

Chapter Two: Free!

I ran out of the cottage before my father could think of another rule to give me. I heard both him and my mother laughing as I hurried out. I was free! Oh yeah, and I had a few rules I had to follow, but I was free!

Once outside, I breathed in the fresh, cool air. Autumn was slowly giving way to winter. You could feel the change in the air. Not many leaves remained clutching to the trees. Soon, the trees would be bare as they waited for the snow to cover their branches. Only the evergreens would remain, filling the forest with their wonderful scent of pine.

I looked around, searching for my friends. As expected, they were waiting just outside the forest. I smiled widely, grateful to have good friends like them. I thought about what my father had just told me, how I had put them in danger. I loved my friends, and I never meant to put them in harm's way like that. I would make it a point to be on my best behavior from now on.

I waved to them. As usual, Cory was flipping his hair away from his face. It only fell back again, but Cory never seemed to notice that. Delia was her usual impatient self. She had her arms crossed in front of her as she waited for me to come out. Her long, dark hair had grown, or was it just me? Even Cory looked a little different; I just couldn't put my finger on what had changed about him.

"It's about time," Delia said, rolling her eyes. "What took you so long?"

They began making their way to me. "We were about to leave," Cory said.

As they neared the cottage, I got the sense that they had grown. Not a lot, just enough for me to notice. I hadn't been in jail that long.

I began counting in my head… *one, two, three, four, five, six, and seven, seven weeks.* I looked at them again. "Why are you looking at us like that?" Cory asked. "I was just kidding about leaving."

Maybe it was just in my head. I really hadn't seen them for more than a few minutes at a time these past weeks. I decided to let it go.

"What have you both been doing while I was in jail?" I asked.

Delia shrugged her shoulders. "Not a whole lot. I go see Miri sometimes."

"You visit her?" I asked surprised.

Miri was one of the humans we had become friends with. I had known Cory was hanging out with her brother, Zachary, but I had no idea Delia was on visiting terms with Miri. I felt a little jealous.

My friends had gone on with their lives while I was being held prisoner. What else had I missed?

"How is Aidan doing?" I asked. "Is he walking yet?"

"And running," Cory answered. "His parents don't suspect a thing. They believe his foot got all better because of the fall they *think* he took."

"Has Miri asked for me?" I asked, putting my head down.

"Of course she has," Delia assured me. "I promised her we would go visit today. She was very excited."

"She was?" I said, shooting my head up.

Maybe I was just being silly. I felt a little left out, but it wasn't Miri's fault I was grounded.

"Enough about them," Cory said, taking my hand. "We have something to show you."

He began pulling me away. "Wait," I said, pulling my hand back.

"What is it?" Delia asked.

"It's my father. He gave me a few rules."

I began telling them the long list I had to follow. They didn't seem surprised one bit.

"Is that it?" Delia asked.

I frowned. "What do you mean, is that it?"

Cory laughed. "Those are the same rules you've always had. You just never listened."

"He also said I couldn't fly," I informed him.

Cory stopped laughing. I knew he'd been waiting eagerly for my punishment to end. I had promised him I would teach him my flying spell.

"What about the spell?" he whined.

Delia rolled her eyes. "It will have to wait, Cory," she hissed. "Thea will get in trouble all over again. She's never been grounded this long."

"Yeah, I suppose your right," he agreed.

I didn't want them to think we could no longer have fun. Magic had been a big part of what we did all the time, I didn't know if we could live without it. One thing I did know, we would have to try. I was never going to put them in danger again, not if I could help it, anyways.

"So what did you want to show me?" I asked.

Chapter Three: Winter Berries

Cory took my hand again and quickly led me away. We headed into the woods and began to follow a path I knew well. We usually took this path when going to our favorite lake to swim.

"Why are we going to the lake?" I asked.

"You'll see," Delia answered from behind me.

Salem's woods were changing fast. The red and yellows I loved so much were quickly fading away. Soon, our favorite lake would be covered in a sheet of ice. Human children would be playing on the snow covered ground of the forest. Humans would be out in full force, chopping wood to get them through the harsh winter.

Those were times I was grateful my father was a wizard. He usually put a spell on the wood to make it burn longer. Sometimes one log would burn for days.

As we walked down the path, I noticed some of the shrubs were already filled with winter berries. The bright red berries were small and hard, but very delicious. Most humans didn't even know they could be eaten.

"These came in fast," I said, pulling one off a shrub.

"That's what we wanted to show you," Cory said stopping.

I was confused. "You wanted to show me berries?"

He shook his head. "No, I wanted to show you what the humans were doing with them."

He grabbed my hand again. He pulled me behind him until we reached a small cottage on the far end of the lake. He motioned for us to be quiet, and then moved closer to the cottage.

I wasn't sure what we were looking for, not until I saw her. There was a woman sitting outside with her children. They had a basket of berries next to them. The woman had a threaded needle in her hand, and she was taking the berries her children would hold out to her.

"What is she doing?" I asked.

"She's stringing the berries," Delia whispered. "She's been doing it for days. They come out every afternoon and fill a basket with the berries."

"But, why?"

Cory pointed to the window. "To put them on the tree," he said.

It was then I noticed a huge tree had been placed by the window. It already had several strands of berries hanging around it.

"I told you they were doing it again," Delia said, nudging me.

I looked at the tree again. Pine cones had been hung all over it. The bright berries made the pine tree look radiant and bright.

"Why do you suppose they do that?" Cory asked.

That was a good question. We had seen the humans doing this before. Strange thing was, they also put wrapped packages under the decorated trees.

"Miri has one, too," Delia announced. "I saw it yesterday."

"Miri has one?" I asked surprised.

She nodded. "And it's even bigger than this one. Cory and I watched her father cut it down."

Her words went through my head; *Miri also had a tree.* Perhaps she could shed some light on our questions. We were friends now, after all, and they knew we were witches. I didn't see any harm in asking her about the trees.

"We should go see her," I suggested.

"She's already waiting for us," Delia said brightly. "I told you, she was excited when I told her you would be visiting her today."

That made me happy. I missed Miri, and I was delighted to hear that she missed me, too.

There was something special about Miri. From the moment she learned we were real witches, she never displayed any fear for us. Other humans would have thrown us in jail for being a witch. But not Miri, she was over the moon about it. In fact, so were her brothers.

I couldn't wait to see her. I wanted to hurry and get to her house. I almost asked Cory to pull down a branch so we would fly, but then my father's voice rang out in my head…"*No flying. You'll put our world in danger.*"

I bit my lip. Now how was I going to get around? As a thought occurred to me, a smile slowly spread across my face. Maybe there *was* something I could do.

"Why are you smiling?" Delia asked nervously. "I don't like it when you do that."

"You have an idea, don't you?" Cory asked.

I faced them both. "My father said *I* couldn't use my magic."

"Yeah, we know that," Delia answered.

I shook my head. "But he never said that *you* couldn't use *your* magic," I pointed out.

I saw the look on Cory's face. I knew he understood what I was saying.

"She's right," Cory said, looking at Delia. "He only gave those rules to Thea."

"He'll kill us," Delia hissed.

"Why would he?" I asked in a demanding voice. "You wouldn't be breaking any rules."

Cory didn't wait for her to answer. He quickly sat and began to pull off his shoes.

I knew this wouldn't put us in danger. Humans run all the time.

"Thea, give me your shoes," Cory said, holding out his hand.

I quickly kicked off my shoes and handed them to Cory. I looked at Delia, "What are you waiting for? Give Cory your shoes."

She shook her head. "What if we're seen? Your father will fry us for sure."

"We're not going to fly," Cory clarified. "We're just going to run—really fast."

Delia was giving it some thought.

"Humans run all the time," I pointed out. "Even if we're seen, that wouldn't be anything strange."

"Yes, it's true," she said, looking away.

She finally agreed and kicked off her shoes. Cory quickly pushed them all together and began to chant his magic at the shoes… "Give us quickness, give us speed; give us all the energy we need. Take our feet and make them fast; make us run with one quick blast."

The moment Cory finished the spell, the shoes vibrated as his magic took effect. I reached for my own pair and quickly slipped them back on.

"Are you sure this won't get us in trouble?" Delia asked as she slipped on her own shoes.

"My father never said we couldn't run fast," I reminded her. "Besides, I didn't use *my* magic, remember?"

Chapter Four: Timber!

Delia finally agreed to run with us. Cory was very excited that I was finally going to try out one of *his* spells. "I never get to use my spells," he said under his breath.

Cory positioned himself ahead of us. "Try to keep up!" he said, launching himself forward.

He was gone in a flash.

Delia and I quickly ran off after him.

I ran as if there was no ground under me. Every step I took felt like a thousand. The shoes carried me so fast that I could hardly see the trees as I past by them. When I had to jump over a log, I was launched twenty feet in the air. This was better than flying. I could jump and almost touch the tops of the trees.

Cory's shoe spell was working wonders. I whipped by trees as the wind blew my hair wildly.

"Thea! Look out!" I heard Delia scream.

Before I could slow down, I heard someone shout, "Timber!"

I heard the sound of something snapping. *Snap, snap, snap,* I heard above me. I finally managed to stop myself and looked up.

"Get out of there!" Delia shouted at me.

In a flash, someone slammed into me and quickly moved me out of the way. The force of the impact threw us about ten feet away. It took me a moment to realize it was Cory. He quickly threw himself over me as a huge tree hit the forest floor.

I felt pine needles hit my face as dust drifted into the air. Then I felt a pair of unknown hands reach for me. "Are you alright, child?" a strange voice asked.

It was a human, with a long white beard and white hair. His rosy cheeks caught my attention. It almost seemed like he had used berries to make them so rosy. I glanced at the axe he was carrying.

"Forgive me," the man said, helping me to my feet. "I didn't see you."

Cory jumped to his feet. "What's the big idea? You trying to kill us?"

The man towered over Cory, but Cory wasn't afraid. "Don't touch her," Cory said, pulling me away from the man's grasp.

"There wasn't anyone here a moment ago," the man explained. "You came out of nowhere."

The human looked down at me. "Are you hurt, little one?"

I shook my head no. I knew it wasn't his fault.

"You almost killed her," Cory said jabbing his finger into the man's chest.

Delia tried to pull Cory away, but Cory kept glaring at the man who was three times his size.

"My apologies, young man," the human said. "I assure you that I meant the girl no harm."

I instantly felt guilty for finding a loop hole in my father's rules. Now Cory was about to get into a fight because of me.

I reached for Cory's hand. "I'm fine, Cory. Can we leave now?"

Cory's eyes finally peeled away from the human. "Are you hurt?" he asked.

"She's fine," Delia said eyeing the human.

Cory reached for my hand, gave the human a dirty look, and led me away.

It was a very quiet walk to Miri's house. We didn't use the shoe spell again. I knew we were all thinking the same thing; humans were everywhere now.

We had always relied of the seclusion the forest offered us. Witches lived undiscovered like that for years. The words, 'deep in the forest' didn't seem to matter anymore. Humans were living closer and closer to us with every passing day. I was starting to see that using my magic really was dangerous.

When we arrived at Miri's house, she was standing outside her house. Zachary and Aidan were with her. "See," Delia said. "She's waiting for you."

I stopped dead in my tracks. There was something different about Miri and her brothers.

"Is something wrong?" Cory asked.

I didn't answer. I couldn't stop looking at Miri. Was it possible that her hair was longer? She looked a bit taller, too. I looked at Aidan and Zachary, and they too, looked taller. Their bangs had also grown. I could hardly see their faces.

"How long was I in jail?" I asked my friends.

"You were *hardly* in jail, Thea," Delia said, rolling her eyes. "You were just grounded for seven weeks."

"And just for an hour a day," Cory laughed.

Although it was true I had only spent an hour in my little corner of the cottage, I had only seen my friends a handful of times. Now I was noticing the changes in them. Miri seemed a bit taller, almost as tall as me. When did that happen? Why wasn't I growing, too?

When Miri saw me, I quickly forgot about my troubles. I was far too happy to think of little else. "Hello, Little Witch," Miri called.

"Miri!" Zachary yelled at her. "Don't call her that—not here."

"Our parents aren't home," she reminded him. "It's okay if I call her Witch."

Miri flipped her hair and ran to my side. "I missed you, Little Witch," she beamed. "I'm happy to see that you're not grounded anymore."

Miri had the most beautiful brown eyes I'd ever seen. Her smile could easily light up the sky. Her hair was so long, much longer than I remembered.

"What's wrong, Little Witch?" Miri asked when all I could do was stare at her.

There *was* something different about her, I was sure of it now.

"I'm just so happy to see you," I answered.

Aidan quickly arrived and asked if we could go flying. I noticed he was walking with no problem. "I'm not allowed to use my magic," I informed him.

"What?" he gasped. "Now what are we going to do?"

"Same thing you always have," Cory snapped at him. "Don't make Thea feel bad like that."

"You didn't even say hello to her," Miri scolded him.

Miri gave me a bright smile. "It's okay, Little Witch. You don't have to use your magic today. There's lots of stuff we can do."

"Like what?" Aidan whined.

"Aidan," Zachary snapped at him. "You're being very rude."

As they argued, my eyes traveled to the small cottage. There, sitting in front of the window, was a decorated tree.

Miri followed my eyes. "Oh, that's our tree," she said. "We're not finished with it yet."

I looked at her. "Not finished?" I asked confused.

She nodded. "We still have to hang our stockings on it. Want to come see it?"

I looked back at the tree. "Yes," I whispered.

Chapter Five: The Christmas Tree

My eyes grew wide as we neared the cottage. Delia was right; this tree was better than the one near the lake. It had so many strands of berries hanging from it. Beautiful burlap bows had been tied onto almost every branch. Delicate candles hung around the whole tree. It truly took my breath away.

Cory and Delia were as fascinated as I was.

"Wow," Cory said, looking up at the giant tree. "It's the best one I've seen."

"Have you put your tree up yet?" Miri asked.

"Do witches even celebrate Christmas?" Zachary added.

"What's Christmas?" Delia asked.

"Are you kidding me?" Aidan gasped. "You don't know what Christmas is?"

Delia shot him a dirty look. "I asked about it, didn't I?"

"So, Santa Claus never brings you anything?" Aidan asked amazed.

"Why should he?" I said. "He doesn't know who we are."

Aidan laughed. "Santa Claus knows who everyone is."

Delia, Cory and I exchanged glances. Who was this guy? And why did he know everyone?

"Well, we've never met him," Delia hissed.

"Is he the one who makes you put up a tree?" Cory asked.

All at once, the humans started laughing. I couldn't understand what was so funny.

"Zap them, Thea," Cory demanded.

Before I could raise my hand, Miri's mother walked into the cottage. I quickly noticed she was holding a basket of freshly picked berries. "Ah, I see your new friends are here," the mother said, placing the basket on the floor.

Miri's mother was a very pretty lady. She had long dark hair like Miri.

"And who are you, little one?" she asked, looking down at me.

"This is Thea," Miri answered for me. "She's my other new best friend."

The mother smiled. "Do you go to school with Miranda?" she asked.

Delia squeezed my hand. I wasn't sure what to say. I had no idea what school was, then I remembered when Zachary said it was a place where you went to learn and stuff.

"No," I answered. "I already learned a bunch of stuff."

The mother gave me a strange look.

"We met them while trick or treating," Zachary explained. "I think they go to another school," he lied.

We all looked at him. That was a *really* good lie.

"Well, welcome to our humble home," the mother said. "Will you be helping us with the berries?"

"They'd love to," Zachary said, winking at me. "Maybe you can tell them the story you told us about Santa Claus and Christmas."

The mother smiled. "You love that story, don't you?"

Zachary nodded. "Very well," the mother said. "Just let me start a fire outside. I'm making stew today."

When the mother left, Zachary leaned closer to me. "I've heard this story a million times," he whispered. "I just said that so you could hear it, too."

Zachary's mother called us outside when the fire was going. "Why don't you sit around the fire," she suggested. "We can string some berries as I tell you the story."

I took my place next to Cory and Delia, who wouldn't look away from Zachary's mother. Miri sat next to me and held out some berries. "Put the needle through the berries," she instructed.

I reached for a needle as her mother began the story. "Once upon a time, there lived a man named, Santa Claus. With his long, white beard, and white hair, he was a very jolly man. There was so much love in his heart, that God blessed him with special powers."

"He has special powers?" I asked, interrupting her.

"He has a long, white beard and white hair?" Cory added.

"Just listen to the story," Miri said, tapping my hand.

We both nodded and her mother continued.

"God awarded him these special powers because he wanted Santa to find the good in us all.

~ 32 ~

That's when Santa Claus thought of a brilliant idea. He would use his *special powers* to watch over all the children of the world. He would keep a list, and check it twice, making sure they were all being good children. And as a reward for their good conduct, he would bring them gifts when they slept at night, thus encouraging them to be good throughout their lives. There's only one problem," she said, leaning toward me. "He had only one night to deliver his gifts."

"One night?" Delia gasped.

She smiled. "As I said, God gave him special powers. He can fly throughout the night and reach every child on earth."

"He can fly?" I asked, as my jaw dropped.

Again, she smiled. "He not only flies, he can also read your heart. He knows when you've been good or bad, he knows when you're asleep. He knows everything about you."

Well, that explained things. No wonder I've never met him. I've broken every rule in the book. I'll never see a gift from him.

"And why the trees?" Cory asked.

The mother looked toward the cottage. "Well, how else will Santa know that we believe in him? I've always told my children that it helps Santa find us."

"The prettier the tree, the faster he comes," Miri said.

"And what kind of gifts does he bring?" Delia asked.

"Whatever you ask him for," Miri said excitedly. "He brings them because he loves us."

"Even witches?" I asked.

"Santa loves everyone," she answered.

"Of course he does," Miri's mother said. "But it's not all about the gifts he brings; it's about how deserving you are. When you ask him for something, he decides how much you've earned it."

I noticed Cory was in deep thought. He was no longer paying attention.

"Are you okay, Cory?" I asked.

He gave me a strange look.

"I'm fine," he said, looking away.

What was wrong with him?

I looked at Miri's mother again as she continued the story.

"What does he use to fly with? Does he use a branch?" I asked hopeful.

The mother chuckled. "No dear, he uses his magical sleigh. Reindeer pull it through the sky for him."

"Reindeer can't fly," Delia shot.

The mother smiled. "Santa's reindeer can. He feeds them magical seeds so they can take him through the sky."

Again, I noticed Cory wasn't paying attention. Something was wrong with him. I listened to the rest of the story as I watched Cory carefully. What was wrong with him? I got the sense that he wanted to leave. Question was, why?

The mother finished telling us about Santa's red suit. She went on about other things, but I wasn't paying attention. My eyes were on Cory.

Chapter Six: It Was Him

We didn't stay for very long. Miri was very disappointed when I said we had to leave. I knew she wanted us to stay for dinner, but I explained how my mother wanted me home early. I really didn't need to leave yet, but the truth was, I was worried about Cory. He looked worried about something. He didn't even bother saying goodbye to Miri or her brothers, and stomped his way into the woods.

"Why are you walking so fast?" I asked him.

"Leave me alone, Thea," he said, waving me away. "Just go home."

"What's your problem?" Delia hissed.

Cory stopped, sighed, and then sat on a log, putting his head down.

"Cory, what is it?" I asked.

"I'll never see a gift from that *Santa* guy," he answered. "He'll never come to my house."

"Don't say that," I said, sitting next to him. "I've never gotten a gift from him either. But I think it's because we've never put a tree up before."

"I ruined my chances, Thea," Cory said, looking away. "He'll never come visit me, even if I put up a hundred trees."

"What makes you say that?" Delia asked.

Cory jumped to his feet, seeming very frustrated. "Don't you see?" he yelled. "I almost got into a fight with that guy. I'm sure he hates me now."

"What on earth are you talking about?" Delia asked.

I froze. I knew exactly who Cory was talking about. Why didn't I catch that?

"It was him," Cory said, shaking his head. "He was the one cutting down that tree today. He had the white beard, the white hair. He even had rosy cheeks, and I was rude to him."

"But he wasn't wearing a red suit like in the story," Delia pointed out. "He looked like a normal man."

"Maybe he wasn't working today," I suggested to Delia.

"It was him, alright," Cory said in a doomed voice. "And I was going to hit him."

"It was a misunderstanding," I said trying to reason with him. "Maybe we can go look for him and explain things."

Cory shot his head up. "You think he'll hear us out?"

"I don't see why not," I answered. "He seemed friendly enough. Why don't we go talk to him? I bet you he's still cutting down trees."

Cory was running through the woods before I could say another word. Delia and I were having a hard time keeping up with him.

"Boy, you *really* want to talk with this guy," I called out.

Cory came to a sudden stop. He faced us with anger in his eyes. "Don't you understand?" he asked. "I have no one. This is my one chance to ask for a family. If this guy really brings you what you deserve, I don't see why he wouldn't bring me a family."

Delia and I exchanged glances.

"I don't think it works that way, Cory," Delia said.

"I have to try," he shot at her.

I felt my heart breaking for Cory. I never knew he felt that way. One thing I did know; I was going to help him find this 'Santa' guy. If he had the kind of powers Miri's mother talked about, I knew he would bring Cory a family.

"Come on," I said, taking Cory's hand. "Let's go find this guy."

Cory finally smiled. "Thank you, Thea."

"Maybe we can ask him for something, too," Delia said as we walked away.

"What would you ask him for?" I asked.

She shrugged her shoulders. "I don't know, but if he can give Cory a family, maybe he can give me a mother."

I thought about what I would ask for. I already had a mother and father. I would have to give this some more thought.

By the time we got back to the spot we had seen Santa, he was gone.

"Now what?" Delia asked.

We decided to check the cottages that were near the area, but luck was not on our side. We didn't find one single house that had reindeer or a sleigh. We almost gave up hope when Delia came up with a brilliant plan.

"Why don't we put up a tree?" she suggested. "Didn't Miri say that the prettier the tree, the faster he comes? We'll make it the best tree ever so he'll come tonight."

It was like a bolt of lightning going through my head. Of course that would work. Question was, whose house would we use to put up a tree? I couldn't do it at my house, my father wouldn't allow it. I was in enough trouble with him.

"We'll put it up at my house," Delia said. "My father is never home. You can both spend the night."

"That's perfect," Cory said, grabbing her shoulders. "We'll wait up for him and explain everything. Maybe he'll forgive me."

I instantly became discouraged. There was no way my father was going to let me spend the night at Delia's house. Today was my first day of freedom, and I didn't want to push my luck.

"I can see you're worried, Thea," Delia said. "Let me handle this. You won't have to ask your father anything. After I bring out the water works, he'll be begging you to spend the night at my house."

"I gotta see this," Cory said, leading the way.

Chapter Seven: Water Works

I could smell my mother's cooking before we reached the cottage. She was making dinner and probably wondering where I was.

I was really hoping this was going to work. I had no idea what Delia was going to say. I planned on staying quiet, just like she suggested.

"What if my father says no?" I whispered.

Delia rolled her eyes. "Trust me, Thea. He's not going to say no. Just let me handle it."

"Thea? Is that you out there?" I heard my mother ask.

"Yes, Mother."

"Come inside. Dinner is almost ready."

I swallowed thickly and the three of us walked into the cottage.

My father was sitting at the table, book in hand. "Well, look who's on time," he said, putting down his book. "You actually listened to me."

"Oh, I don't plan on breaking anymore rules, Father."

He laughed. "I certainly hope not."

He looked at Cory and Delia. "Will the two of you be joining us for dinner?" he asked.

"Of course they will," my mother said, placing two more plates on the table. "I won't take no for an answer."

"Thank you," Cory said, pulling out a chair.

As Delia and I sat, my father put his book away and asked about our day.

"What kind of trouble did the three of you get into today?" he asked playfully.

When Cory cleared his throat, I was shocked at the words that came out of his mouth.

"Miri's mother told us a story about a man named Santa Claus," he blurted out.

My jaw dropped.

"Ahh, the gift giver," my mother said from the stove.

"You know about him?" Cory asked surprised.

"I know the legends," she answered. "I've always wondered if they were true. I always assumed they were human tales."

"I've heard them as well," my father said. "The humans seem to make quite the fuss over him this time of year."

"Did you know he has special powers?" Cory asked. "He grants wishes."

My mother placed some food on the table and sat next to me. "That's silly," she said. "Why would a man grant wishes to us?"

"Not to you, Mother," I quickly informed her. "He only grants wishes to children, and only if they've been good."

"I see," she said, glancing at my father. "And I suppose you're all wondering why he's never granted you a wish?"

"It's not a wish," Delia said, rolling her eyes. "He brings gifts. You ask him for something, and he brings it."

"How is that possible?" my mother asked.

"Because he has special powers," I explained. "And he brings his gifts all in one night."

My mother looked at my father. "Did you hear that, William? The humans make a fuss over a man that has powers, and they're not even scared of him. In fact, they even wait for him."

My father laughed. "We should be so lucky."

They both chuckled. My mother served us all her special stew and we began to eat. As my father reached for some bread, he asked if we would share what we had learned about Christmas and Santa Claus. He paid close attention as Cory explained why Santa Claus had powers. When Cory was done telling him the story Miri's mother had told us, my father looked intrigued.

"Now I understand why they put up trees," he said, shaking his head. "I suppose if it helps children behave, there's no harm in believing."

"Don't you believe, Father?"

He looked at me. "I'm not sure, Thea. It seems a bit farfetched that a man has that kind of power and only uses it to bring gifts. Someone like that can't be real."

I put my spoon down. "But you have powers, and you're real."

My mother raised one eyebrow and looked at him. "She has you there, William."

He smiled at her. "So tell me," he said, looking at us. "If the legends are true, what would you ask him for?"

"People," I answered.

"What?" my mother laughed.

"Not for me," I explained. "They're for Cory and Delia."

My father looked confused. "I don't understand, Thea. What kind of people?"

"You know, a mother and father. But I think we'll need two mothers, one for Cory and one for Delia."

Both my parents looked at Cory and Delia.

"I see," my father said.

I saw a tear run down my mother's cheek as she looked away.

There was silence. Then Delia began to cry. I instantly got nervous. Was this part of her plan, or was she really crying? My mother quickly gathered her in her arms.

"I want to put up a tree," Delia sobbed.

"Of course you do, sweetie," my mother said, holding her tight. "We'll cut one down for you tomorrow. Won't we, William?"

"Y…yes, of course we will," my father said not knowing what to do.

"No," Delia said, shaking her head. "I want a tree tonight. It has to be tonight. Santa won't bring me a mother if we don't put it up tonight."

My mother quickly shot my father a look. "William, go cut her down a tree this instant."

"Where will be put it?" he asked. "There is no room for it here."

"We'll put it outside if we have to," my mother hissed at him.

"No," Delia cried harder. "It has to be in my house. I want it there."

"And there it shall be," my mother said, stroking her face.

Chapter Eight: Is He Here Yet?

Before I could make sense of what had just happened, my mother was packing me an overnight bag. She swiftly sent my father next door to inform Sharron that Cory would also be coming with us.

As for me and Cory, we were both in awe of Delia's acting skills. The moment my mother agreed to let me spend the night, Delia's tears had disappeared. She even winked at me before laying it on a little thick with my mother again. She also somehow managed to get my father to cut down the tree for us.

"Man, she's good," Cory whispered as my father cut down the biggest tree he could find.

"I've never seen anything like it," I answered.

Delia was very smug. She would flip her hair and almost pat herself on the back. She even made my father pick a basket of berries before we headed to her house. I was truly in awe of her.

And just as Delia had said, her father wasn't home when we arrived at her house.

"Of course he's not home," my father mumbled under his breath.

My father dragged the tree inside and placed it near the window. We all stood back and looked at the giant beauty. "I think it's too big," my father said, taking a step back.

"No," Delia said beaming up at it. "It's perfect.

"We have to string the berries," Cory said, grabbing the basket. "We don't have much time."

My father sighed and ran his fingers through his hair. "Is this what you really want?" he asked us.

Delia's eyes instantly became watery. "Miri said, the prettier the tree, the faster he comes. I just know he'll bring me a mother."

Man, I had to take some lessons from her.

My father looked at the tree and sighed again. "I need you to understand something," he said, facing us. "This tree may not work the way you think it does. Even if this 'Santa' person comes, he may not be able to give you what you're looking for. Are you prepared to accept that?"

"He will come, Father. You'll see."

He was thoughtful for several long moments. He finally smiled and faced the tree.

"I can't believe I'm doing this," he said, waving his hand toward the tree.

His magic began to flow throughout the tree. I was amazed when long icicles began to form on the branches. He waved his hand again, and sparkling stars appeared all over the tree. It was as if he had pulled them right out of the sky. He looked down at the basket of berries, and one by one, they began to scatter themselves all over the beautiful tree.

"It's breathtaking," Delia said amazed.

When my father was done, he turned and faced us again. "I shall not be the one who takes away your hope," he began. "But if this tree does not bring you what you seek, promise me you will never let go of that hope."

We all looked at the tree. "We promise," we all said in unison.

My father ran his fingers along my face before quietly walking out the door.

"How did he do that?" Cory said, touching one of the stars. "They're filled with light."

"This tree will make him come for sure," Delia said. "I don't think there's another tree like it."

"We should get ready for him," I suggested. "Cory needs to apologize right away so he doesn't leave."

In a flash, we began to scout the house. This was going to be hard. The house had only this room, with Delia's bedroom off to one side. We decided to hide under the dinner table. It was big enough to fit all three of us. We also had a clear view of the tree form there.

We quickly put our blankets under the table as Delia threw a tablecloth over it. Cory lay down, put his pillow under his elbows, and kept his eyes on the tree. I scooted next to him with Delia by my side. We were ready; we would jump out as soon as Santa walked in and explain things. I planned on telling Santa that Cory meant no harm. I needed him to understand that Cory was just trying to protect me.

"Man, that tree is lighting up the whole house," Delia whispered. "It's so beautiful."

"That's why he *has* to come," Cory answered.

"Stop talking," I hissed. "He might hear us."

"How does he get here, anyway?" Delia asked. "Does he just walk through the door?"

"Maybe he just appears?" I suggested.

"I think Thea is right," Cory agreed. "He has powers, remember?"

We looked at the tree again. "He's *really* going to like that tree," I said.

"Does he take the tree with him?" Delia asked.

No one knew what to say. That was a good question. "I think he does," Cory said.

"Wow, he must have a lot of trees," I answered.

We kept our eyes on the tree as we waited for Santa to arrive. A minute turned into an hour. An hour turned into two. My eyes were becoming heavy. I was having trouble keeping them open. I began nodding off, but Cory nudged me with his elbow. "Stay awake, Thea. He'll be here any minute."

I yawned and tried to make out the tree. My vision was blurred. I wanted nothing else but to fall asleep. Delia was already snoring next to me. Her last words had been, "Is he here yet?"

When I opened my eyes again, it was daylight. Cory and Delia were still sleeping. Poor

Cory had fallen asleep sitting up. His head was leaning on one of the table legs.

I quietly scooted out from under the table. I walked up to the tree and wondered why Santa hadn't liked it. It was a pretty tree, there was no doubt there. My father had done a fine job of making it sparkle. I just couldn't understand it. Why didn't he come?

I began to realize that we would have no choice but to go out looking for him. He had to come out sooner or later. I had to tell him that Cory didn't mean to be rude to him. He just had to forgive him.

"He didn't come, did he?" Cory asked.

I hadn't heard him get up.

"No," I said, looking up at the tree again.

"He's angry with me, Thea. He'll never come."

"Then we'll go to him," I answered.

Cory looked out the window. "It's not going to be easy finding him. It's already snowing."

Chapter Nine: We Did It Wrong

Cory and I watched the snow fall as Delia snored the morning away. We agreed to go back to the same area where we had first seen Santa. Today we would play the waiting game. I was prepared to use my magic if I had to. If Santa wouldn't hear us out, I planned on freezing him until Cory could apologize.

When Delia finally woke up, she was surprised to see it was snowing.

"Did he come?" she quickly asked.

There was no need for us to answer, our faces told her everything. "We'll try again tonight," she assured us.

"Thea and I already have a plan," Cory said. "We're going to him."

"But it's snowing outside," Delia answered.

When Delia looked out the window, she made an odd face. Cory and I quickly turned to see what she was looking at.

"Is that Miri?" Cory asked.

"Who's that girl she's with?" Delia asked, moving closer to the window.

It really was Miri. She was all bundled up in a very pretty coat. There was a little human girl with her. She was very thin and frail. She had long, curly brown hair and thick eyebrows. They kept looking toward the house.

"What are they staring at?" Delia asked.

It took me only moments to realize they were staring at the tree. I knew I could easily explain to Miri how we got the stars to light up, but who was this girl? I couldn't tell her my father had used magic. Who was she?

"What do we do?" Cory asked.

"I'll go out and talk to her," I said, heading for the door.

A cool breeze hit my face when I opened the door. The outside world was quiet. I loved the silence of a fresh snowfall. Everything was quiet and muffled. I always thought it sounded like cotton balls coming down from the sky.

"Hello, Little Witch," Miri said when I walked out.

I instantly looked at the stranger and shook my head at Miri. Why was she calling me 'Witch' right in front of her?

"It's okay, Little Witch," Miri explained. "She can't hear me. She's deaf."

I looked at the little girl again; she was only staring at the tree. She must have been about eleven years old. Miri quickly introduced her to me.

"This is my cousin, Abigail. They're visiting us for Christmas. She lost her hearing when she was a baby."

Miri looked at the tree. "That is a beautiful tree, Little Witch. Santa will stop here for sure."

"The tree didn't work," Cory hissed from the door. "We waited all night, and he never came."

Miri laughed. "Last night wasn't Christmas, silly. Santa only comes out one night a year, remember?"

Cory and I quickly looked at each other. Of course, we did it wrong, and on the wrong night.

"When is Christmas?" Cory asked.

"Tomorrow," she answered.

Miri looked at the tree again. "Did you use magic on the tree?" she asked. "Because if you did, you should close your curtains. Trees aren't supposed to light up like that."

In a flash, I heard Delia closing the curtains. She was obviously listening to us.

"Open," Abigail mumbled.

"Oh, she likes the tree," Miri said, smiling at her.

"She really can't hear us?" Cory asked.

"Not a word," Miri answered. "But she can speak a few words."

The little girl kept staring at the window, hoping we would open the curtains.

"Open," she mumbled again.

"No, we have to go now," Miri said, grabbing her hand. "Mother is waiting on these eggs," she said, holding up a small bag.

Miri waved goodbye to us and pulled Abigail behind her. Abigail looked over her shoulder until they disappeared down the road.

"I can't believe we did it wrong," Cory said, slamming the door behind us. "I can't wait another day to speak with him. He'll be too busy."

"Let's go looking for him now, before it snows too much," Delia said, reaching into her chest of clothes.

Cory began to gather his things as Delia looked for something warm to wear. I was about to head toward the table to gather my blankets when Delia tossed a dress on the floor. "What's that doing in there?" she said.

I looked down at the dress; I had seen it before. My mother had given Delia this dress when she saw the one she was wearing was torn. I remember it well because it was one of my favorite dresses. Why didn't she want to wear it anymore?

I reached down and picked up the dress.

"Don't you like this dress anymore?" I asked, holding it up.

Delia took a quick glance at it. "Yes, but it doesn't fit me anymore."

I looked at the dress again; I could easily wear it with no problem. It would fit me just as well as it had fit me a year ago when my mother gave it to Delia.

I held up the dress as my eyes examined Delia. She was right; this dress was too small for her. She had grown.

I left my friends and stepped into Delia's room. It was more like a nook, rather than a room. Just a small little bed could fit in here. I threw the dress on the bed and removed my clothes. I reached for the dress and slipped it on. It fit perfectly. I hadn't grown an inch.

I felt paralyzed as I began to realize what this meant. I wasn't aging. I was going to stay a little girl forever.

I began to think of what my mother had told me weeks before. She said we stayed in hiding because she didn't want humans to notice how slow I was aging. Had she lied to me? Did she not want to tell me that I would never age?

I tried to sort through my memories. I tried to think of the days when Delia and I were the same height. Now I could see it; I really hadn't grown.

"Are you coming or what?" I heard Delia call.

Chapter Ten: The Barn

I walked out of Delia's room feeling numb. I didn't bother putting my other dress back on and walked out. Delia didn't seem surprised to see my old dress on me.

"Oh, look at that," she said. "It still fits you."

I looked at her with new eyes. Her hair had always been as long as mine, but now I could see hers was longer. I looked at the dress she was wearing. It was full of patches from where my mother had sewn it. Now I understood; my mother wasn't trying to fix her torn dress, she was trying to make it fit her for as long as possible.

I could see where she had tried to lengthen the dress, adding patches to make it longer.

"What's wrong with you?" Cory asked.

I slowly looked at him. My eyes traveled down to the bottom of his pants. There, sewn onto the hems, were my mother's patches again.

"Thea, what's wrong with you?" Delia asked. "Why are you just standing there?"

I felt a wave of panic flow through me. All I could picture were my friends outgrowing me and moving on with their lives. I would be left all alone. They would die of old age, while I was left behind without them.

I couldn't imagine my life without Cory and Delia in it. Who would I play with? Who would run with me in the woods I loved so much?

"Thea?" Delia said, moving closer.

My panic rose and I made for the door. I threw it open and ran away as fast as I could.

"Thea!" I heard Cory shout.

I wasn't sure where I was going; I only knew I needed to be alone. A million questions were going through my head like: Did my friends know I wasn't aging? Why hadn't my parents told me? Most importantly, *why* wasn't I aging?

My feet carried me into the forest until Cory's voice faded. I knew he would be running after me soon, so I reached for a branch, pulled it down, and held it up. "Fly," I commanded.

A gust of wind blew under me as I put it between my legs and was carried away. I couldn't feel the effects of the cool morning air. I didn't even care if human eyes spotted me flying. I was heartbroken. I was going to lose my friends one day. My eyes filled with tears as that thought went through my head.

I wasn't aware how long I had been flying, but when I stopped, I had no idea where I was. It felt like hours had passed as I wandered through the woods feeling heartbroken. I was covered in snow and soaking wet. I finally found a barn and decided to take refuge in it. I threw myself on a pile of hay, closed my eyes, and began to cry.

I was too scared to go home. I didn't want to hear the truth I had already figured out. Nothing my father could say would make me feel better.

I cried myself to sleep as I shivered from the cold. Hours passed and I stayed in that little barn. I somehow convinced myself that if no one told me the truth, it would never happen. Time would never pass, and my friends would never outgrow me. I slipped into a deep sleep thinking of them.

I was awakened when someone suddenly opened the barn doors. Cool air quickly filled the place. I wrapped my arms around myself and tried to sit up. My head felt like I had banged it against a wall. My body was achy. I couldn't stop the shivering cold that was going through me. I somehow felt hot, but knew it was freezing. I wanted nothing else but to fall asleep again.

"Who's in here?" a voice said.

At first, I could only see the lantern the stranger was holding up. "Answer me!" the stranger shouted.

"I...I'm not stealing anything," I answered.

The man quickly moved the lantern my way. I was shocked to see who it was. It was him, it was Santa Claus. "What on earth?" Santa said when he realized it was me.

"What are you doing here, little one?" he said, putting the lantern down next to me.

He quickly removed his coat and wrapped it around me. "You're soaking wet," he said, rubbing my shoulders.

I could hardly keep my eyes open. I felt so weak. "Why didn't you come last night?" I mumbled. "You would have liked our tree."

"You're burning up," Santa said, lifting me up into his arms.

From the corner of my eye, I caught the glimpse of a sleigh. It was filled with wood and not gifts, but I knew Santa wasn't working today.

"I need to speak with you," I said, leaning my head on his chest.

I was barely aware that we were moving. All I could feel was the cold that was making me shiver. Then I heard it, a voice from not far away. "Thea!" It was my father, he was searching for me.

"Over here," Santa called. "I think I found what you're looking for."

"Oops," I said in a weak voice. "There goes another seven weeks."

I heard my father's frantic voice, a moment later, I felt him gathering me in his arms.

"What happened?" he asked in a demanding tone.

"I'm not sure," Santa answered. "I found her in my barn. She has a bad fever. She's burning up."

I felt my father's cold fingers on my face.

"You'll be the death of me, Thea."

"Quick, bring her inside," Santa suggested. "I have a fire going."

"Is she okay?" It was Cory.

"Go fetch her mother," my father ordered. "Tell her to bring dry clothes."

"Yes, Sir," Cory answered.

My father held me close as he carried me into the cottage. Santa quickly offered my father a blanket to wrap me in.

"Please," my father said. "Can you throw more wood into the fire?"

"Yes, of course," Santa answered. "I'll go to the barn and fetch some now."

The moment Santa walked out, my father held me closer and whispered, 'heal', into my ear.

Instantly, his magic made me feel warmer. The shivering stopped and I opened my eyes. My father sighed and held me to his chest. "What am I going to do with you, Thea?"

He kissed my head and leaned back, holding me close to him. I could feel his heart racing. His hands shook as he wrapped more blankets around me. I could tell he was trying to catch his breath.

Santa soon returned and quickly threw a few logs into the fire. "How is she doing?" he asked.

"The fire is helping," my father answered.

There was silence. All you could hear was the crackling of the fire. I finally dared to look into my father's green eyes. "I'm sorry," I whispered.

He held me closer. "We'll talk when we get home," he answered.

He was still breathless. I felt bad for making him worry like that. I looked at Santa; he smiled and asked if we would like some hot tea.

"That would be nice, thank you," my father answered.

My father kissed my head again. "How are you feeling?" he asked.

"Warmer," I whispered.

"I love you, Thea."

I looked up at him. "Even now?"

I was glad to see him smile. "Nothing can make me love you less. You will always be my little girl."

I almost gasped when he said that. Had I just found the reason why I wasn't aging? Did my parents want me to stay their little girl forever? I knew my father had that kind of magic. Keeping me young wouldn't be a problem for him.

I looked away as Santa returned with two cups of hot tea. Before he could offer my father a cup, my mother came bursting through the door. "Thea," she cried.

Chapter Eleven: Wake Him Up

I was quickly enveloped in my mother's arms. She put me on my feet and cried as she kissed my face over and over again. "My little girl," she kept repeating.

I froze when she said that. So I was right; she was in on this, too. They both wanted me to stay a little girl forever. Now I knew I *had to* speak with Santa.

Cory stood near the door, a look of shock on his face. He kept staring at Santa. I knew he was realizing who it was.

"Should I fetch a doctor?" Santa asked. "She's burning up."

I realized he had no idea my father had already used his magic on me. The fever was all but gone. "What?" my mother said, touching my cheeks.

My father cleared his throat. "She's feeling much better now," he said, giving my mother a subtle nod.

She understood at once. "That won't be necessary," she answered. "The fever is already going down," she said, eyeing my father.

Why were they trying to hide the fact that my father had used magic? Santa knew all about magic. We didn't have to hide it from him.

"My father has powers, like you," I informed him. "He made it go away."

"Thea!" my father gasped.

My mother pulled away from me. "You shouldn't say such things, Thea. The gentleman will think you've gone mad."

"It's probably the fever talking," Santa said nodding at my father.

"Yes, of course it is," my father quickly agreed.

"You made it go away, Father. I'm feeling much better now."

"Thea, please don't say such things," my mother said, eyeing Santa Claus.

"Did you bring dry clothes?" my father asked her.

When my mother nodded, he suggested she change my clothes and get me home—right away.

My mother quickly pulled me into another room and removed my damp clothes. "Please stop talking," she said, as she dressed me.

She threw my wet clothes into a bag and quickly grabbed my hand. "Off we go," she said, pulling me behind her.

"Why do you want me to stop talking?" I asked.

"Please, Thea. Just stay quiet."

Cory was still standing near the door when we returned. He wouldn't take his eyes off Santa. "May I have a word with you?" Cory asked nervously.

Santa looked at him. "Yes, of course."

Cory stepped forward. "I want to apologize for being rude to you the other day. I didn't mean to upset you. I had no idea who you were."

Santa studied Cory's face. "Oh, now I remember you," Santa answered. "You have a bad temper, young man."

I pulled my hand away from my mother's.

"He was only trying to protect me," I explained. "It was my fault. You should be angry with me."

"What is this all about?" my father asked.

Santa faced him. "I'm afraid I almost dropped a tree on your daughter the other day. I was cutting wood and they came out of nowhere. The young man here was kind enough to scold me for it."

"I'm sure it was an accident," my father said.

"I didn't mean it," Cory assured him. "Honest, I didn't know who you were."

"And who do you think I am?" Santa asked.

"You're Santa Claus," Cory announced.

There was a confused look on Santa's face. I had to explain why we didn't know who he was. I couldn't leave without speaking with him first.

"I can explain everything," I said, taking a few steps closer to him. "We didn't know about Christmas. We're witches, you see. And we sort of hide from humans."

"Thea!" my mother gasped.

I spun around and faced her. "It's okay, Mother. He has powers, too. He can also fly."

"Witches?" Santa said, eyeing us all.

"Yes, but my father is a wizard," I said, pointing at him. "That's how he was able to make the fever go away so fast."

My mother quickly shot a look at my father. "Do something, William."

~ 69 ~

My father quickly crossed the room and tapped Santa on the head. Santa closed his eyes and bowed his head.

"Why did you do that?" I yelled. "I needed to speak with him."

My father knelt down and grabbed my shoulders. "Thea, I don't think this man is who you believe him to be. He's just a human. You can't go around telling people what we are."

"Santa doesn't care if we're witches," I answered. "Miri said he loves everyone."

"This isn't Santa," my father hissed.

"Yes, he is," I cried. "He's just not working today. I was going to ask him for a wish."

"This man is human, Thea," my father repeated.

"Wake him up," I cried. "Please, wake him up. I have to ask for my wish."

"Enough," my father yelled.

He sighed and rose to his feet. "Take them home," he said to my mother. "I'll clean things up here and be home shortly."

My mother nodded and we quickly headed out into the night. I knew my father was going to erase us from Santa's memory. Santa would never remember we had met. Then a thought occurred to me; Santa would also never remember Cory had been rude to him. That would solve one problem, but I still needed to speak with him.

I knew my father was wrong about Santa. Miri had explained how adults really didn't believe in him anymore. I could see my father was one of those adults. I knew Santa's magic only worked if you truly believed in him. I knew that was him, it just had to be. I would have to find a way to come back and ask for my wish.

When we made it back to our cottage, Delia was waiting outside for us. She was already shaking her head at me.

"Come inside," my mother said passing her.

"What did you do now?" Delia asked as we walked inside.

"We found him," Cory whispered to her.

"Who? Santa Claus?" she asked surprised.

"Yes, and Thea's father just erased his memory."

"What are you talking about?"

"I believe Sharron is waiting for you," my mother said to Cory. "Why don't you go home now. Thank you for your help today."

Sharron was a witch that lived next door. She had taken Cory in when his parents passed away.

"I'll see you in the morning," Cory said, waving goodbye.

"Your mother doesn't sound happy," Delia whispered.

"Delia," my mother said. "Why don't you wait for Thea in her room? You can sleep here tonight."

Delia and I exchanged glances before she slipped into my room. My mother pointed toward the dinner table and told me to have a seat.

"Your father and I need to speak with you," she said in a stern voice.

Chapter Twelve: The Wish

My mother made a fire as we waited for my father to return. She hardly said two words to me the whole time. She hung a pot of water over the fire and sat next to me.

"Don't you ever do that to me again," she said, putting her hand over mine.

I knew she wouldn't understand my reasons for wanting to speak with Santa. It was clear she didn't believe in him, either. She only wanted me to stay a little girl forever, I was sure of it now.

I didn't care if they punished me for this; I wasn't going to let that stop me. I was determined to have words with Santa. He would understand my need to keep growing, and remove this spell my father had cast on me.

I swallowed thickly when my father finally walked in the door. He was covered in snow and soaking wet. My mother was quick to help him remove his coat. "Sit by the fire," she said, draping his coat over a chair.

"It's starting to really come down out there," he said, holding his hands up to the fire.

"I'll make you some tea," my mother said, reaching for the pot.

"Thank you, Emma," my father answered.

I waited quietly for the punishment I knew was coming. I wanted to get it over with and go to bed. I had a long day tomorrow. The walk to Santa's cottage wasn't a short one. I knew I wouldn't be able to fly.

When my father warmed up, he sat across from me at the table. My mother put a cup of hot tea in front of him and took a seat next to him.

My father's hair was still soaking wet. I noticed a few strands of gray hair that were already growing. It was nice to see that *he* didn't mind aging.

"So how many weeks am I grounded for this time?" I asked.

"Excuse me?" my mother asked shocked.

"You watch your tone with us, young lady," my father added.

I put my head down and didn't answer.

"How did you meet this man?" my father asked.

"I was running through the woods with Cory and Delia," I explained.

"And, were you using magic?"

I bit my lip. "Yes," I admitted.

"Yes, what?" my father said, raising his voice.

"Yes, Father."

"What has gotten into you, Thea?" my mother asked. "Why did you go looking for this man?"

I didn't answer.

"Your mother is speaking to you," my father yelled.

I looked up. "I didn't go looking for him. I was lost. I found him by accident."

"And what is this nonsense about speaking with him?" my father asked. "What can you possibly have to say to him?"

I sighed. "I wanted to ask him for a wish," I confessed. I slowly put my head down again.

"Thea, what kind of wish?" my mother asked.

I glanced at her. "I don't want to tell you."

My parents looked at each other.

"But why?" my father asked. "Why don't you just ask us for your wish?"

I began to fidget. Why would I ask them for my wish? They would never give me what I was asking for.

"Thea?" my father said softly. "If you have questions about something, why don't you just ask us?"

I bit my lip. I knew my answer was going to get me in trouble. "Because I know you'll lie to me," I finally answered.

You could hear a pin drop. My parents did nothing but stare at me. I began to wonder how many weeks I would be kept inside this time. The list of chores I would have to do was already going through my head.

"I see," my father said, leaning back in his chair. "And you're sure of this?"

I nodded. Again, they did nothing but stare at me. "This man is a human, Thea," my father said. "He has no powers. I just need you to understand that. The legends about him are a myth, fairytales made up by humans. And I assure you, that is no lie."

I slowly looked up at him. "I know he's real, Father. Just like I know you're real. You just don't believe in him."

Frustrated, my father rose to his feet.

"Go to your room," he said, pointing. "I will not hear another word about this mythical man that doesn't exist."

Huge tears welled up and ran down my cheek. "He's real, Father. You'll see."

"Thea, go to your room," my mother said with a big sigh.

I quietly pulled out my chair and headed to my room. Delia was biting her nails when I walked in. "I heard every word," she said.

I didn't answer and plopped myself on my bed. "What happened tonight?" she asked.

I looked at her and decided I needed to know something. "Did you know I wasn't aging?" I asked, wiping my tears away. "And why didn't you ever tell me?"

Delia leaned back. "What?" she asked confused. "What on earth are you talking about?"

"You really didn't know?"

"Know what, Thea?"

"That I wasn't aging?"

As her eyes traveled up and down my body, I realized she really didn't know. In fact, she seemed rather shocked.

"Why didn't I ever notice that?" she murmured.

I decided to tell her everything, even the events that took place tonight. She agreed that it was my parents that wanted to keep their little girl forever. "What other reason could they have for not letting you age?" she said.

"That's why I need to speak with Santa," I explained. "He'll know what to do."

"But I thought your father erased his memory. What if he doesn't remember you?"

"I have a plan," I whispered. "And I think Miri and her brothers can help us."

"What can they do?" Delia asked.

"Don't you see, Delia? They know all the rules when it comes to Santa. They can tell us if we're doing something wrong."

"That makes sense," she agreed.

We both jumped when my father opened the curtain that separated my room from the dining room. "Blow out that candle," he said in a voice full of poison. "There will be no staying up for you tonight."

"Yes, Father."

He turned to leave. "And another thing," he said, facing me again. "We've decided not to punish you this time. You may come and go as you please. If you get yourself in trouble, you will have to deal with the consequences. I will not be looking after someone who thinks I'm a liar."

He turned on his heels and walked out. I felt horrible the moment those words left his mouth. I never meant to call them liars; I only meant to say that I knew they wouldn't tell me the truth. Wasn't there a difference?

I blew out the candle and jumped into bed. Delia pulled the blankets over her head and was snoring in no time. As for me, I couldn't sleep. I kept thanking my lucky stars that I wasn't punished. Tomorrow, I would go look for Santa and ask for my wish.

Chapter Thirteen: They Left Me

The morning brought new hope. I jumped out of bed feeling excited. Although my parents were upset with me, I knew I was doing the right thing. They would have to except the fact that I was going to grow up one day.

I shook Delia until she opened her eyes. "Get up," I said, pulling the blanket away. "We need to get out of here before my father changes his mind."

She stretched and yawned. "Is it morning already?"

I began to search for warm clothes. "You go next door and explain to Cory what the plan is. Ask him if he wants to come with us."

Delia sat up. I could tell she didn't want to get up. "So you stay a little girl for a while. What's the big deal?"

I shot a look at her. "Don't you care if I stay young forever? How will we look playing together when you look like my mother?"

Delia gave my words some thought. After a few moments, she jumped out of bed.

"There's no way I'm going to be confused for your mother," she said, reaching for her clothes.

She dressed in a flash and hurried next door to speak with Cory. I made my way out of my room—slowly. My mother was making breakfast. I spied a plate of eggs already waiting for me on the table.

"Morning," my mother said in a cold voice.

"Good morning, Mother."

I looked around for my father. "He's not home," my mother said, pouring me some milk. "He left early this morning."

I was surprised when she placed the milk on the table and walked out of the cottage. I wasn't sure what to do. I suddenly felt guilty for hurting their feelings. That was never my intent. My mother was clearly angry with me.

I forgot about my eggs and hurried out the door. I had to tell her how sorry I was. How could I blame her for wanting to keep me a little girl? I knew it was out of love. Didn't I want to be with my friends for the same reason?

I was starting to realize that calling my parents liars had been a mistake. There wasn't anything they wouldn't do for me. What was I thinking? I'm sure there was a good explanation for what they were doing. I should have told them; I should have asked them about it.

And where had they gone to? My mother left in such a hurry. They had never left me alone like this. My father's words suddenly went through my head... *"We've decided not to punish you this time. You may come and go as you please. If you get yourself into trouble, you will have to deal with the consequences. I will not be looking after someone who thinks I'm a liar."*

"They left me," I whispered.

What had I done? I drove my parents away. I was a monster. "Mother?" I called.

It had stopped snowing. There was a fresh blanket of snow on the ground. Everything sparkled and shined. Normally, the fresh snow would have made me run around with joy, but now I felt nothing but sorrow.

"Mother?" I called again.

She was nowhere to be found. I couldn't even see her footsteps in the snow. Where had she gone? Was she coming back?

"Cory is getting ready," Delia said running up to me. "He's in."

Once again, panic began to rise inside of me. I had hurt the two people I loved most in the world. I just had to do something. I turned and grabbed Delia's shoulders.

"Tell Cory to meet me at Santa's house," I said. "He knows how to get there."

"Why don't you just wait for him?"

"There's no time. I have to catch him before he leaves."

I ran into the woods before Delia could ask another question. In a matter of seconds, I had cut down a branch and was flying through the air.

I knew I was breaking the rules again. Flying through the woods in broad daylight was one of the first things my father told me not to do, but this was an emergency. I had to speak with Santa, now more than ever. He had to bring my parents back to me.

I was careful to look out for human eyes as I flew to Santa's house. It was a bright sunny day, and the sun was beaming off the snow, giving me perfect cover. I knew the snow would keep most humans indoors, and I was too deep in the forest to run into the kids.

I flew unworried. My only mission was to reach Santa. I was willing to beg, if needed, in order to get my parents back. I knew my father had left, but I wasn't sure about my mother. One thing I did know, I wasn't taking any chances.

I came to a sudden stop when I heard someone yell… "Timber!"

I heard a tree hit the ground. I quickly jumped off my branch and began to search the woods. At first, I could only see a sleigh full of wood. Then I saw him, it was Santa. He was cutting down trees again.

He didn't have on his red suit, but I knew he wasn't working today. I took a deep breath, swallowed thickly, and made my way to him.

Chapter Fourteen: Run Along

As I moved closer, I was surprised to see a horse strapped to Santa's sleigh—and not a reindeer. Shouldn't he be filling it with gifts by now? I looked at the sleigh; it wasn't what I was expecting. It looked old and worn. It wasn't shiny like Miri had described it. This sleigh didn't look like it was anywhere near ready to fly.

"Is this a flying horse?" I asked.

Santa spun around. He seemed startled.

"You scared the dickens out of me, child," he said, grabbing his chest.

"Oh, I'm sorry. I didn't mean to." I looked at the horse and, he too, looked old and worn.

"Does this horse turn into a reindeer?" I asked. "He looks very tired."

Santa looked at the horse, making an odd face. He shook his head, "Be off with you, little one. I have work to do. The early snow put me behind. So, run along." He began chopping the tree he had just cut down.

"I need to speak with you," I said, moving closer. "I have a wish to ask for."

Santa swung his axe into the tree. "Do I look like I grant wishes?" he asked.

I was quickly reminded that it wasn't a wish. It was supposed to be a request.

"Oh, I'm sorry. I mean, I have something to ask you for; something I need you to bring me."

Santa swung his axe again, leaving it in the tree. He dusted off his clothes as a smile broke across his face. "I think I know what this is about," he said, putting his hands on his hips. "I'm afraid you've come to the wrong person, little one. I am not the man you think I am."

I looked at his white beard and his white hair. "Aren't you Santa Claus?" I asked.

He chuckled. "I'm afraid I only look like him. But I assure you, I am just a normal man."

"Oh, no," I whispered.

The truth was right in front of me. I just couldn't believe it. My father had not only erased me from Santa's memory, he had also made Santa forget who he was.

"Now, run along," Santa said. "I have a long day ahead of me."

Santa waved me away, picked up his axe, and returned to his wood chopping. This was horrible. I couldn't leave and do nothing. Kids all over the world were counting on him. I had to help him remember.

"You are Santa," I proclaimed. "You just can't remember who you are."

Santa sighed. "I don't have time for this."

"Please," I said, moving closer. "Let me explain. Just give me a moment of your time."

He shook his head and put the axe down again. "Let's have it," he said, facing me. "What is it you need to explain?"

"You see," I began. "My father was angry with me because I told you I was a witch. But I think he was angrier that I told you he was a wizard. Anyway, he erased your memory because he doesn't believe you're Santa Claus. The bad thing is, I think he erased too much. Now you don't know who you are."

Santa just stood there, a confused look on his face. I was surprised when he got a little angry with me. "I don't have time for this nonsense. Can't you see I have a lot of work to do? Now, be off with you."

He turned and mumbled something I couldn't make out, shaking his head the whole time. He began chopping the tree into smaller pieces. I could see it was going to take him a long time. An idea quickly came to me.

"You want me to do that for you?" I offered. "It will only take me a few seconds. Then, you'll have time to speak with me."

He laughed, but didn't stop chopping. "I'd like to see that," he answered.

"Okay," I said, waving my hand.

In an instant, the tree began cutting itself into perfect logs. Santa froze when the logs began stacking themselves neatly on his sleigh.

"Is that where you wanted them?" I asked.

Santa stood, completely frozen; his hand still clinging to the axe. He slowly backed away as the axe slipped through his fingers.

"Will you be cutting down another tree?" I asked. "Or do you want me to do it?"

I couldn't understand why Santa was breathing like that. It almost seemed like he couldn't catch his breath.

"Are you okay?" I asked concerned.

He backed away more and more. Before I knew it, he was running.

"Where are you going?" I called.

He began running faster. What had gotten into him? I quickly reached for a branch, jumped on, and began flying after him. It didn't take me long to catch up to him. "Why don't you jump on my branch," I said, flying next to him. "I can take you where you want to go."

I was confused when Santa started screaming. He had such a look of horror in his eyes. What was scaring him?

"Get away from me!" he shouted in a terrified voice.

What was I thinking? Of course Santa would be scared. He didn't know he was Santa. This was all new to him. He couldn't remember that magic was real. I had to find a way to calm him down.

I waved my hand, sending my magic right at him. Santa screamed some more when his feet left the ground. He was lifted into the air and floated right next to me. "Please stop screaming," I said. "The humans might hear you."

Again, a screeching, terrifying scream came out of his mouth. I became worried when he started turning white.

"Leave me, you evil demon," he shouted.

"That's not very nice," I scolded him. "I'm just a regular witch."

More screams filled the air. I had to silence him. I knew the humans would hear him sooner or later. "This won't hurt," I said, waving my hand.

"Please, no!" he screamed before my magic put him to sleep.

This was going to be harder than I thought. I would have to take Santa back to his cottage and work on restoring his memory. Problem was, I didn't know how to do that. My father had never shared that spell with me.

Chapter Fifteen: He's Not?

It didn't take me long to get Santa back to his cottage. It was actually quite easy. I just made him float the whole way. I already had a nice fire going. The cottage was nice and warm. I still couldn't find where Santa kept his tea. I knew a nice hot cup would calm him down.

I had him sitting on a chair. I decided to tie him down so he wouldn't run away again. It was unfortunate that I had to put something over his mouth. He just wouldn't stop screaming. Every time I stood in front of him, that terrified look would come back.

"Where do you keep the tea?" I asked from the kitchen. "I can't find it anywhere."

Santa only mumbled. I quickly remembered he couldn't talk. I crossed the room, stood in front of him again, and pulled down the scarf.

"Where is the tea?" I asked again.

His face trembled as he looked into my eyes. Huge tears ran down his face as his lips trembled. After a moment, he began screaming again.

I quickly put the scarf over his mouth again. I decided to just sit and explain things to him.

"This will be over soon," I said, but that only made Santa kick and squirm.

"Don't be scared," I said, placing my hand on his knee. "The others will be here soon."

I thought his eyes were going to pop out of their sockets. He began to shake his head.

It was obvious he wasn't going to calm down, so I took a seat on a footstool and began to explain things to him.

"I want to ask for my wish before my friends get here," I explained. "You see, I found out I wasn't aging. It really bothered me at first, but I think I'm okay with it now. But the bad thing is, I called my parents liars, and I think they both left me. At first, I was going to ask you to make me age again, but now I only want my parents back. I feel horrible for hurting their feelings. So, you see, I need you to bring them back."

A knock at the door interrupted my discussion with Santa. He tried screaming through the scarf, but I quickly put my finger over my lips.

"It's just my friends," I assured him, but that didn't seem to calm him.

"Thea, are you in there?" I heard Delia say. "I brought Miri, Zachary, and Aidan like you wanted.

I waved my hand and the door flew open. Delia walked in first, with Cory, Miri, Zachary, and Aidan right behind her. Even Abigail had come with them.

"You scared him," I said as they walked in.

"What the...?" Cory gasped.

Santa was struggling to break free. I had to put him to sleep again when he wouldn't stop.

Everyone seemed shocked for some reason. They walked in slow, jaws on the floor. I couldn't imagine how this must have looked to them.

"He kept screaming," I explained. "I had to tie him up."

"Thea, what on earth are you doing?" Delia asked.

Why was she looking at me like that?

"I was talking to Santa," I answered. "My father erased his memory, and now he can't remember who he is."

Zachary, Miri's brother, shook his head.

"Thea, this isn't Santa."

I looked at Santa, and back at Zachary. "Yes, he is. He just can't remember who he is."

Miri, who still had her jaw on the floor, moved a little closer. She put her hands up and swallowed thickly. "Little Witch, you can't do things like this. You'll get in horrible trouble. This man isn't Santa."

"He's not?" I asked, looking at him.

"Santa lives at the North Pole," Aidan said from behind her.

"What's the North Pole?" I asked.

Miri moved closer to me. "That's where Santa lives," she said nervously. "But it's only a story, Thea. It's not real. It was only a story."

"What?" I asked confused.

"Let me handle this," Zachary said, pushing Miri behind him.

He moved closer to me. "You didn't hurt him, did you?"

Why would he ask me that? I would never hurt anyone. "Of course not," I answered. "He's only sleeping."

Zachary nodded; seeming relieved I hadn't hurt Santa. "Thea, you know that story my mother told you about Santa?"

I nodded. "Well, it really is just a story," he explained. "We've known for years that Santa isn't real. It's just something adults tell us so we'll behave. But Santa doesn't exist."

His words flowed slowly through my head. *Santa doesn't exist?*

Cory and Delia looked as surprised as I did.

"Why would your mother lie to us?" Cory hissed at him. "It's obvious Thea believed her."

"What about the trees?" Delia asked.

Zachary became nervous. "Let me explain," he began. "No one has ever seen Santa before. Although millions talk about him, there's no proof he's a real man. I mean, how can one person have the power to deliver that many gifts in one night?"

"Did you know witches were real?" Cory shot back. "You didn't believe in magic either, not until you met us."

"That's true," Delia said.

Zachary didn't know what to say. He knew Cory was right. "Listen," Zachary said. "To be honest with you, we're too old to believe in Santa anymore. We only listen to those stories to please my parents. But I don't believe in him anymore."

"So this isn't really Santa?" Cory asked.

Zachary put his head down. "No."

There was silence. I felt my heart breaking into a million pieces. I was trying to accept the truth, but my heart didn't want to hear it. I couldn't understand why so many would talk about a man that wasn't real. It didn't make any sense to me. There had to be some truth to the stories. Even my parents have heard about Santa.

"Well, that would have been good to know yesterday!" Delia shouted.

Out of nowhere, Abigail ran to the man I thought was Santa and sat on his lap. She pointed to her ears and shook him. "Wake up," she mumbled. "Hear," she said, pointing to her ears again.

I instantly knew she was asking Santa to restore her hearing.

"No, Abigail," Miri said, pulling her off Santa's lap. "That isn't Santa."

I looked at her. "Are you sure?"

Aidan answered for her. "I told you, Santa lives at the North Pole. If this was Santa, he'd have a red suit around here somewhere. And there would be reindeer in the barn."

Miri nodded, agreeing with Aidan. "And Santa would also be saying, ho ho ho," she added.

Suddenly, Cory crossed the room. He knelt down and grabbed my shoulders. "Thea, why don't you wake this man up? We'll erase his memory and go looking for the real Santa. I'll search all night if I have to, but I really don't think this is him."

My lips began to quiver. I was on the verge of tears. "It has to be him, Cory. Who's going to bring my parents back?"

"What are you talking about?" he asked.

"They left me," I said, breaking into a sob. "I called them liars and they left me."

He laughed and pulled me into his arms. "Thea, they would never leave you. They adore you. You're everything to them."

"Thea, why do you think they left you?" Delia asked.

I pulled away from Cory. "Because my mother said my father was gone, and when she cooked me breakfast she left, too."

Delia started laughing. "You are so impulsive," she said, shaking her head. "You're mother only went next door to ask if we wanted to have breakfast with you. I didn't tell you because you left in such a hurry. I had no idea you were looking for her."

"She didn't leave me?" I asked as my heart came alive again.

Delia rolled her eyes. "Talk about jumping to conclusions. Get a grip, Thea."

"Thea," Cory said, grabbing my shoulders again. "Erase his memory so we can get out of here. We shouldn't be here."

"I don't know how," I admitted. "I can wake him up, but I don't know how to erase his memory."

"Oh, that's great," Delia said, rolling her eyes again.

Cory rose to his feet. "I'll go get Sharron. She'll know what to do. You all wait here."

"What about him?" Zachary asked, pointing at the phony Santa.

"Leave him there," Cory said, heading for the door. "Sharron will take care of it. I won't be long. I'll use my shoe spell."

"Your what?" Miri asked confused.

Cory was out the door and didn't answer. Everyone looked at me when Cory slammed the door behind him. "Never a dull moment with you around, Little Witch," Miri said, shaking her head.

Chapter Sixteen: Doomed

I knew I was going to be in big trouble when Sharron arrived. She would no doubt rat me out to my father. I would have to sit in my little corner for months this time. My friends would probably me married and with children before my punishment was lifted.

"You know, Thea," Miri said from the couch. "If you went to school, you'd know all about these things."

We were all sitting on the floor, all of us but Miri, of course. She had been lecturing me on how impulsive I was. Abigail was wandering the cottage, unaware of what was going on.

Delia was rolling her eyes as Miri continued her lecture. "In school," Miri said, "they teach you all sorts of…"

"We don't know what school is," Delia said, cutting her off.

Before Miri could answer, there was a knock at the door. "That must be Sharron," Delia said, jumping to her feet.

Delia froze half way to the door when an unfamiliar voice came from the other side.

"Lucas, are you home?" a voice called.

All at once, we gasped. Miri quickly jumped off the couch. "Oh, no," she whispered.

The man knocked again. "Lucas, we found your horse and sleigh in the woods. Is everything okay?"

I bit my lip. I had completely forgotten I had left Santa's things behind. Zachary began waving his hands at us, motioning to stay quiet.

"Lucas," the man said, pounding on the door. "Are you hurt?"

We didn't know what to do. We couldn't let these men in and see the phony Santa. I thought of waking him up, but he would only tell his friend about my magic. "Quick, Thea," Delia whispered. "Erase his memory."

"I don't know how," I reminded her.

"Kick it open," I heard another voice say. "Hurry."

Zachary quickly tried to untie the phony Santa. "They can't see him like this," he said, but it was too late.

The door flew open when one of the men kicked it so hard it almost flew across the room. Five men stormed in, axes in hand. Judging by the clothes they were wearing, I could see they, too, had been cutting down trees.

They looked like giants, almost as tall as the trees. Well, it seemed like that to me, anyway. They were a bit stunned to see a bunch children staring back at them. "Whatever you do," Zachary whispered to me. "Don't use your magic."

The five men scanned the room, then they saw him. We still had the phony Santa tied to a chair. He was sound asleep. I knew in that very instant, we were doomed.

"What the devil is going on?" the younger of the five asked. "Why is old Lucas tied up like that?"

One of the men, a red haired one, ran to the phony Santa and tried to wake him. "Lucas," he said, shaking him. "Are you alright?"

"He's just sleeping," I explained. "I didn't hurt him."

"Thea, shut up," Zachary said, eyeing the men.

"Why is he tied up like this?" the red haired man asked, pulling out a knife.

He quickly cut the ropes and put the phony Santa on the couch. He tried to wake him, but my magic kept him sound asleep.

"I didn't hurt him," I repeated. "I just put him to sleep."

"Thea," Delia hissed. "Stay quiet."

Another man, this one bold and fat, stomped his way to me and grabbed my shoulders. "What do you mean, you just put him to sleep? What did you do to him?" he asked, shaking me.

"Leave her alone," Delia screamed.

"Answer me!" the fat man said, shaking me again. "I'll beat it out of you," he threatened.

"You're hurting me," I said, trying to pull away.

"I think they've killed him," the red haired man said, backing away from the phony Santa.

"What?" the fat man gasped.

He pushed me away and began to shake the fake Santa. "Lucas," he kept saying.

My magic was too strong. I knew the only way for him to wake up was for me to do it.

The other men surrounded us as the fat man attempted to wake his friend. Miri began to cry, which only made Delia cry.

"You really don't think these children killed him, do you?" the red haired man asked.

"Well, they did something to him," the fat man shot back. He glared at me, his eyes full of poison. "And I'm about to find out what," he said, unstrapping his belt.

"Wake him up!" Zachary yelled at me. "Quickly, before he hits you."

I didn't think twice. I waved my hand at the phony Santa, and he opened his eyes.

"He's awake," the red haired man yelled.

The moment phony Santa realized his friends were there, he looked around, took a deep breath, and shouted... "She's a witch!"

He quickly sat up and pointed right at me.

"Witch!" he shouted again.

Delia's screams sent a surge of panic right through me. I waved my hand again, sending all five men, including the phony Santa, crashing into the wall.

"Run!" Zachary said, pushing us towards the door.

We ran into the woods as quickly as we could. I couldn't run fast enough. I kept looking over my shoulder to see if the men were coming after us. "Cut down a branch," Delia yelled. "We have to get out of here."

Zachary and Aidan stopped, reached for some branches, and quickly handed them to me. I waved my hand, and within seconds, the wind was blowing under us as we flew away.

Chapter Seventeen: Witch!

I tried to catch my breath as we whipped by the trees. I had really gotten us into a pickle this time. Now those humans were going to tell everyone about us. I knew my father was going to be furious with me—again.

We began to slow down when we got a good distance away. "That was a close one," Miri said, jumping off my branch.

She began to whip her head in every direction. What was she looking for?

Oh, no," she said, putting her hand over her mouth. "We left Abigail back there."

"What?" Zachary gasped.

Miri's eyes spilled over with tears. "They're going to hurt her," she cried.

In a flash, I was flying back to the cottage. I ignored Delia's screams to come back and hurried to help Abigail. The thought of someone hurting her made me fly faster. I could only think of that fat man removing his belt.

I would take a million lashings if it meant saving that little girl. Once again, I had put everyone in danger because of my stupidity. I had to get her out of there.

It was odd how I didn't feel any fear washing through me. When it came to my friends, it seemed nothing scared me. I would face an army of belt holding fat men if I had to. I wasn't going to let them hurt Abigail.

The men were outside when I arrived back at the cottage. I was careful to stay behind a tree as they brought Abigail outside. "You're going to tell us where they live," the fat man said, pulling her behind him.

Abigail seemed confused by what was going on. I knew she couldn't hear what the men were saying, and the men had no idea she couldn't hear. They kept asking her questions, and yelling when she wouldn't answer.

Frustrated, the fat man sat Abigail down on the snow and began to ready a carriage. Where were they planning on taking her?

I tried to get Abigail's attention. I needed her to make a run for it so we could fly out of here.

"Abigail," I whispered. "Run this way."

I bit my lip when I remembered she couldn't hear me. I looked at the men; they were busy strapping the horses to the carriage. This was my one chance to rescue her.

I waved my hand and sent my magic right at her. When two sparks came out of her ears, she quickly put both hands over them. "Abigail," I whispered again. "Run this way."

I knew she could hear me now, but why wasn't she running to me. "Abigail, over here," I called, and still, nothing.

She pulled her hands away from her ears and looked around. When she heard the horses, she gasped. With every sound she picked up, she would only gasp and look amazed.

"Hear," she mumbled.

"She's mumbling a spell?" one of them said.

"Silence her," the fat man shouted.

"No, stop!" I yelled, coming out from behind the tree. "She's not a witch," I informed them. "Please don't hurt her."

The phony Santa shot his head my way.

"Witch!" he said, pointing at me again.

The fat man grabbed Abigail and held her close to him. He was quick to put his hands around her neck.

"If you use your magic," he growled. "Your little friend here will pay."

"Please don't hurt her," I repeated. "Take me instead. I'm the witch."

Abigail kept putting her hands over her ears. I instantly knew all the new sounds were hurting her ears. It didn't help that phony Santa kept yelling. "You're hurting her," I said, moving closer.

I thought of waving my hand, but I couldn't take a chance on them hurting Abigail.

When I put my hands up, the red haired man quickly ran and tied my hands behind my back. "You're going to jail for being a witch," he hissed.

"Please, let her go," I begged. "She didn't do anything."

"Silence, Witch!"

"I only wanted to speak with Santa," I cried.

The man tied the ropes to the point that I couldn't feel my hands anymore. Why did they hate me so much? I was just a witch, I wasn't a monster. "You're hurting me," I cried.

"Get your hands off my daughter!"

It was my mother, and Sharron was with her. My mother ran and blew a white powder in the man's face. He instantly looked dazed and confused. Within seconds, Sharron also began blowing powder around. A cloud formed around the men as they became dazed. The fat man tried running, but the powder soon reached him and he froze.

"I cast a spell and take your day," my mother chanted. "Remember nothing and be on your way."

The men closed their eyes and bowed their heads. "Sleep," Sharron said, blowing more powder at them. Soon, they were on the ground and snoring.

I knew my mother didn't have the kind of magic my father did, but she knew some very strong spells.

My mother quickly removed the ropes and pulled me into her arms. "Are you alright?" she cried.

"I just wanted to speak with Santa," I said, throwing my arms around her. "I thought you left me. I thought you didn't want me anymore."

My mother pulled away. "Why on earth would you think that?" she said, brushing the hair away from my face. "You're my world, Thea. I would never leave you."

"I'm sorry I called you a liar," I cried.

She pulled me into her arms again. "All is forgiven, my love."

I only cried in her arms. Her warmth covered me like a soft blanket. There was no other feeling in the world. I could feel her love wrapping itself around me. "Mother," I cried.

"We don't have much time," Sharron said, heading into the cottage. "They won't stay sleeping for long."

My mother nodded. "Wait here, Thea."

Chapter Eighteen: Between Us

I wiped my tears away as my mother headed into the cottage, taking Abigail with her. They had put her to sleep in a flash. After a few minutes, my mother came back out. "Tell me everything," she said, grabbing my shoulders. "What happened here today? I must leave things as they were."

I nodded and began to explain what happened. When I told her the men had come because they had spotted Santa's horse and sleigh in the woods, she quickly sent Sharron to retrieve them.

"Put everything back in the barn," she ordered Sharron.

Sharron was gone in a flash. My mother walked to the edge of the woods and called for Cory. "You can come out now," she yelled.

When Cory came out, he looked angry that my mother had made him wait in the woods. I knew he wanted nothing more than to help her. He would have taken on all those men if she let him.

"Come inside," my mother said to him. "Help me put the house back in order. We'll have to drag these men back inside."

"Yes, Ma'am," Cory answered.

I could only stand there as my mother fixed all my mistakes. She placed things so the men would think they had been together all along. Although I deserved it, she didn't yell at me once.

Sharron was soon back, giving me the evil eye as she put the sleigh back into the barn. She and Cory dragged the men into the cottage. She wouldn't stop giving me the evil eye.

"Trouble maker," I heard her mumble under her breath.

When all bases were covered and my mistakes fixed, I heard Sharron and my mother having words. Cory was sent outside, giving them some privacy. Of course, Cory quickly waved for me to come closer. We put our ears to the door and listened.

"You have to do something about her, Emma," Sharron was saying. "She'll get us all killed one day."

"I plan on speaking with her when we get home," my mother answered.

"Why don't you plan on spanking her instead? She needs a good spanking."

"Don't tell me how to raise my child," my mother hissed.

"William will hear about this," Sharron shot back.

I knew it! I knew Sharron was going to rat me out to my father. She was dying to spill the beans to him.

"I can't believe she wants your mother to spank you," Cory whispered.

I swallowed thickly. I knew this time Sharron may just get her wish.

"I will deal with my husband," I heard my mother say. "This is a family matter."

"You can't be serious!" Sharron said. "Look what she did today. She's out of control. Just give her a good spanking and be done with it."

"Man, she's out for blood," Cory said, shaking his head.

"She's just a child," my mother answered. "And she is *my* child. I won't allow you to interfere with my decision."

"Very well," Sharron answered. "I'll keep this between us. But if she gets out of hand, I *will* speak with William."

Cory and I jumped back when Sharron opened the door. She glared at me and stormed off into the woods.

"Come home after you help them," she hissed at Cory.

"Yes Ma'am," Cory answered.

I couldn't believe my luck. My mother was actually thinking of *not* telling my father about this. My life wasn't over. There would be no punishment or yelling. Better yet, I wasn't going to get a spanking.

"Boy," Cory said, shaking his head again. "You are one lucky witch."

I was speechless. I knew my mother was usually on my side, but this was big. She didn't seem upset with me in any way. I couldn't be that lucky.

I looked back into the cottage and saw my mother deep in thought. She seemed out of sorts somehow. Something was bothering her.

"Mother?" I said walking in.

She looked away from me. "Please, wait outside," she said, wiping her tears. "I need a moment."

I didn't realize she was crying. What was wrong with her? "Why are you crying?" I asked.

"I'm not crying," she lied.

She desperately tried to hide her tears from me. She cleared her throat and wiped away her tears again. "Delia told me why you came here," she finally said.

"But I was wrong, Mother. You didn't leave me. Delia told me you were just next door."

"No," she said, looking away. "She told me the real reason you came here. You wanted to ask Santa to make you age again."

"Oh," I said, finally understanding.

How could I tell her I was okay with it now? It really didn't bother me anymore. I knew my friends would outgrow me one day, but I could make new ones. If staying a little girl is what my parents wanted, I was willing to give them that gift. That would only mean I could keep them forever, too.

"I want you to know something," my mother began. "We have a very good reason for keeping you a little girl. I just can't tell you yet."

She looked down at her shaky hands. "It's not time for you to learn the truth. Soon, your father and I will sit you down and explain things.

But until then, I need you to keep this between us. Don't tell your father you know."

How could I say no? If it meant he would never learn what I'd done, I would keep this secret forever. "I promise," I answered.

She looked around the cottage. "Let's not tell him what happened here today, either. It will be our little secret, understand?"

I smiled. "I double promise," I quickly answered.

I wasn't sure what reason my parents had for not allowing me to age, but it didn't matter anymore. Whatever the reason was, I knew it was for my own good. If there was something I was sure of, my parents loved me, unconditionally and with all their heart.

My mother picked Abigail up from the couch; who was still sleeping.

"Let's get you home now," she said, walking past me.

Chapter Nineteen: Christmas Eve

It didn't take us long to get home. My mother instructed me to cut down a branch so we could fly home. Cory was shocked that my mother allowed me to use my magic, and my mother was shocked at how well Cory could fly.

"Have you been practicing?" she asked him, her eyes on me.

"Our little secret?" I smiled sheepishly.

"What am I going to do with you, Thea?" she said, shaking her head.

"Why don't you spank her?" Cory teased.

I pushed him playfully. "Why don't we tell Sharron to spank you?" I answered.

"That woman is out for blood," Cory said, shaking his head.

"She's just scared," my mother explained. "She worries too much."

"And she's a horrible cook," Cory said, making a sour face.

We laughed about Sharron all the way back home. Delia, Miri, and the others were waiting outside our cottage when we arrived. My mother handed Abigail off to Zachary, who seemed relieved that we had rescued her.

"She'll wake up before you get home," my mother assured him.

"What about those men?" Zachary asked.

My mother smiled. "They will only remember a good game of cards."

"Wow," Aidan said. "I wish I could do that. I'd make my father forget the list of chores he gave me."

My mother laughed. "You should get home now," she said. "Isn't today a special day?"

"It's Christmas Eve," Miri answered. "And we're having a special dinner." She looked toward our cottage. "Too bad you didn't put up a tree. Santa might miss your house."

"I thought he wasn't real?" I shot.

She looked at me. "After today, I believe in everything, even the Easter Bunny."

"What's the Easter Bunny?" I asked.

I thought Zachary's eyes were going to come out of their sockets. "Shut up, Miri," he quickly said silencing her. "Don't give her any ideas."

He was quick to wave goodbye and they disappeared into the forest. What was their hurry?

Delia kept shaking her head at me. "You'll be grounded for months," she whispered.

"I'm not even in trouble," I informed her.

"Says who?" she laughed.

She stopped laughing when my mother asked her if she wanted to go for a walk with us. I had to admit, I was also surprised. Taking a walk was the last thing I thought my mother would want to do. I was even more surprised when she asked Cory to come with us.

"Um, okay," Cory said eyeing me.

I shrugged my shoulders, letting him know that I was as confused as he was.

"We'll have to hurry," my mother said. "It will be dark soon."

She headed off into the woods. "Are you coming?" she called.

Cory, Delia, and I just looked at each other. I shrugged my shoulders again and followed behind my mother.

When my mother heard us, she looked over her shoulder and said, "Look for a tree you like."

"A tree?" Cory asked confused.

My mother stopped, looking up at the trees.

"Didn't you hear? It's Christmas Eve," she answered. "I do believe we're supposed to put up a tree for Santa Claus."

"But it wasn't Santa," I reminded her.

She smiled. "Yes, but that doesn't mean the real one isn't out there somewhere."

"So you believe the stories?" Delia asked.

My mother looked thoughtful for a moment. "When I was a little girl," she began, "I also heard the legends of Santa. I never really knew much about him, only that he brought gifts to children all over the world. I suppose if his legend has lived for so many years, there has to be some truth to it, don't you think?"

She looked up at the trees again. "Now, let's pick out one of these trees, shall we?"

We all smiled at each other. I realized we were about to have our first Christmas. Cory found the best tree in the forest and pointed it out.

"This one is the best," he said.

My mother agreed and asked me to cut it down. I looked at her confused. "I didn't bring an axe," I pointed out.

"Did you bring your magic?" she asked, looking at the tree.

I couldn't believe it. I *actually* had permission to use my magic. Delia had a look of shock on her face. "Well?" Cory said. "What are you waiting for?"

I waved my hand and watched as the tree was gently pulled away from its roots. Cory and Delia began to pick berries. "It's going to be the best tree yet," Delia said.

My faith in Santa was restored. I believed in him again. Even if he didn't come tonight, I knew he was real. If only the thought of someone like him made people act with kindness, then he was real enough for me.

Chapter Twenty: Christmas

My mother went next door when we got home. Cory brought the tree inside while my mother asked Sharron if she wanted to join us for dinner. Cory wasn't happy about it and truth was, neither was I.

I knew Sharron didn't like me. She ratted me out to my parents every chance she got. Cory was upset because he feared Sharron would help my mother cook. He made a sour face just thinking about it. "It's bad enough she snores," he whined.

Cory sometimes slept outside because of Sharron's snoring.

"We're supposed to be kind on Christmas," Delia scorned us. "It's called, 'Christmas spirit.'"

Cory and I felt guilty the moment she said that. We would have to think of something nice to say when she got here.

"I'll be right back," Cory said, heading out the door. "I shouldn't have said that about Sharron," he said over his shoulder.

"Where is he going?" Delia asked. "We have to decorate the tree."

We had placed the tree right by the window. And since I had permission to use my magic, I waved my hand and made the berries string themselves.

"Put stars on it," Delia said excitedly.

I didn't want my tree to look like hers. If Santa came tonight, I didn't want him to think I was a copycat.

I looked outside and an idea came to me. I waved my hand and filled the tree with snow. The light from the candles made it sparkle just as bright as Delia's tree. It was simple, but perfect. It reflected the woods I loved so much.

My mother returned and said Sharron would be right over. She gasped when she saw the tree.

"Oh Thea, it's perfect," she said.

She began to sort through what little food we had. There wasn't much, but my mother somehow managed to cook up a feast.

It was the best night ever. Sharron even managed to smile a few times. We laughed and talked about the humans and all the things we still didn't know. I asked about the Easter Bunny again, but Sharron quickly said, "Don't get any ideas."

It was a perfect night. The only thing missing was my father. Where had he gone?

When my mother cleared the table and served up some sweet bread, Cory pulled something out of his pocket and walked up to Sharron. She was holding a cup of coffee up to her lips, but put it down when she noticed Cory standing next to her.

"Yes?" she said with questioning eyes.

Cory looked nervous. "Um, I don't know much about Christmas," he began. "I do know that it's a time of giving. And I wanted to give you this," he said, holding something out.

He had something wrapped in a piece of cloth. Sharron took it and slowly began to unwrap it. I couldn't see what it was, but it made Sharron gasp when she looked at it.

"It belonged to my mother," Cory explained. "It's the only thing I have of hers. She couldn't wear it anymore because it's broken, but I wanted you to have it."

Sharron became teary. "Are you sure?" she asked him.

Cory nodded. "You're the only mother I have now. And I don't think I've ever thanked you for taking me in."

Sharron was speechless. She began to sob as she held up what Cory had given her. It was a beautiful pin. It had a copper owl sitting on a branch made of brass. A beautiful silver moon sat behind it. The pin was broken, but I quickly waved my hand and repaired it.

Sharron seemed shocked that I had fixed it.

"Thank you," she cried.

She turned and threw her arms around Cory.

"I will treasure it always, dear."

After that day, Sharron was a little less annoying to us.

Chapter Twenty One: Not Even a Mouse

We helped my mother clean up and sat around eating sweet bread. It was getting late, and I was surprised my mother hadn't made us go to bed yet. Cory and Delia were spending the night, and we planned on waiting up for my father.

"He should be home soon," my mother said.

Sharron had gone home, still crying from Cory's gift. I noticed my mother kept looking toward the door. I knew she was worried about my father. Where had he gone?

"Did you ask her what school was?" Delia asked. "We can't go if we don't know what it is."

We were talking about Miri, and this place she called 'school'.

"What do they do in school?" Cory asked.

"They learn," I answered.

"Yes, but learn about what?" Delia asked.

"I think about Santa," I answered. "Because Miri said if I went to school, I would know about these things."

We talked way into the night. I was having trouble keeping my eyes open. When I started nodding off, my mother said it was time for bed.

"You'll see your father in the morning," my mother said, sending us to my room.

Cory took his usual place on the floor. My mother already had blankets waiting for him. Delia jumped in bed with me, and started snoring moments later. How was she able to fall asleep so fast?

"Remember, our little secret," my mother said before walking out.

"Goodnight, Mother. And thank you for making today so special."

She smiled. "I love you, Thea."

I curled up and thought about Miri. I couldn't help but wonder what this school thing was. Maybe I would spy on her and find out. And with that thought, I drifted off to sleep.

I was sound asleep when I heard the faint sound of bells. At first, I thought I was dreaming, but then I heard them again.

"What is that?" Cory said, sitting up.

"You heard it, too?" I asked.

"Did you hear bells?" Delia said, waking up.

We all looked toward my doorway. My mother had lit some candles. I could see the light coming from the other room. "You're home," I heard my mother say. "I was so worried."

"It's your father," Cory whispered.

"How long have they been asleep?" I heard my father ask.

"An hour or so," my mother answered.

I saw the light moving closer to my room. Suddenly, my father peeked in, a candle in his hand. "Thea, are you awake?"

I sat up. "Yes, Father."

He smiled and walked in. He was covered in snow. He lit the candles in my room and asked Cory to sit on the bed.

"Yes, Sir," Cory said, hopping on the bed.

Was I in trouble? Had my mother changed her mind and told my father what happened? I instantly became nervous.

My father stared at the three of us. "I want to thank you," he began. "It seems the three of you always seem to teach me a lesson. I think I'm growing rather used to it."

We looked at each other. "I don't understand, Father."

He smiled. "Your words hit me hard, Thea. You said that I also had powers, and that I was real. Those words affected me so much, that I went searching for something."

"What did you go searching for?" I asked.

He sighed. "I suppose I went searching for the power of believing; the same power you held on to so much. And what I found has changed the person I am."

"What did you find?" I asked.

He smiled and looked toward the door. "You may come in now," he called.

A soft scent of sugar cookies brushed against my face. I breathed deeply when a man dressed in a red suit and red hat walked in. His beard was white as snow, his hair like puffy clouds in the sky. His eyes twinkled like stars, his lips red as the berries on my tree. He wore black boots with a silver buckle, his red suit plush velour. His cheeks had a perfect rosy tint to them. He smelled of vanilla and candy, and when he spoke, his voice was that of an angel. "Hello, Thea," he said in his musical voice.

I drew breath. "You're Santa," I gasped.

When he laughed, a booming, "Ho ho ho," came from his lips.

His belly jiggled as he held it. The room was quickly filled with his sweet breath.

"You're real," Cory gasped.

Santa looked at him. "And so are you," he answered. "Much to my surprise," he added.

"I'll go tend to the reindeer," my father said.

"They like hot cocoa," Santa informed him.

"Of course they do," my father said, shaking his head.

Santa pulled up a chair and sat down. He patted his lap and said, "Who's first?"

I wasn't sure what he was talking about. Santa seemed to understand at once. "You have to sit on my lap if you're going to tell me what you want," he explained.

Delia stormed out of bed and onto Santa's lap. "I want a mother," she quickly said.

Santa smiled. "I'm afraid you'll have to ask for something you don't already have."

"But I don't have a mother," Delia answered.

"What does a mother mean to you?" Santa asked her.

Delia thought about it for a moment. "Well, a mother takes care of you," she answered. "She cooks and takes care of your clothes. She worries when you're not feeling well, and she loves you."

Santa touched her nose. "I do believe you already have someone like that."

"I do?" Delia asked confused.

"It's my mother," I said realizing who Santa was talking about. I looked at Cory. "And you already have a family. You have us."

"Yeah," Cory said with a big smile. "I already figured that out."

"So," Santa said to Delia. "What can I bring you?"

Delia thought some more. She snapped her finger, leaned in, and whispered in Santa's ear.

"Ho ho ho," he laughed. "A wise choice," Santa said.

Delia jumped off his lap. "Are you next, young man?" he asked Cory.

Cory seemed uncomfortable about sitting on Santa's lap, but did it anyways.

"And what can I bring you?" Santa asked.

Cory also leaned in and whispered in Santa's ear. "I see," Santa said. "I'll see what I can do."

It was finally my turn. I began to panic when I couldn't think of what I wanted. I already had my parents back, and staying young didn't bother me anymore. What could I possibly ask for?

"Thea, it's your turn," Cory said.

I nodded and sat on Santa's lap. The scent of vanilla flowed through me. He was a soft as cotton. "What can I bring you?" Santa asked.

I gave it some thought. When I thought of Zachary, Aidan, and Miri, I knew exactly what to ask for.

I leaned in, "I want to never stop believing in you," I whispered.

Santa leaned back. A beautiful smile broke across his face. "I do believe that is the first time someone has asked for that," he said.

He tapped my nose. "But I'm afraid only you have control over that. I live as long as you believe, little one."

"I will always believe," I answered.

I leaned in and whispered something else in his ear. "Ho ho ho," he laughed. "I think I can arrange that."

I jumped off Santa's lap and he rose to his feet. He was magnificent. How could I confuse the phony Santa for him? There was no confusing the real Santa.

We followed him out of my room to find my mother holding out a cup of hot cocoa for him.

"What a fine looking tree," he said taking the cocoa. "I do believe I've never seen one quite like it."

He looked at my mother. "I feel I owe you an apology for not visiting your home sooner, Madam. I'm afraid I was as surprised to learn you existed as your husband was to learn about me. I thought I could sense everyone."

"No apologies needed," my mother answered. "And, thank you for coming today."

Santa chuckled. "Much like you, I had to see it with my own eyes."

He put the cocoa down. "I must be off now. I want to wish you and yours a very Merry Christmas."

"Merry Christmas, Santa," I said.

"Merry Christmas," Delia and Cory repeated.

He touched my nose and walked out. We ran to the door, but he was gone. "Where did he go?" Delia said, running out.

I saw my father holding a cup of cocoa; he was looking up at something. "Thank you, again," my father said waving. "And remember, if you ever need a favor, I'm here."

"I may just take you up on that," I heard Santa say.

I quickly ran out. Where was he? My jaw dropped when I looked up to the sky. Santa was flying away on his sleigh, being pulled by nine beautiful flying reindeer. It was the most magical night of my life.

"Merry Christmas to all, and to all a goodnight," Santa sang.

The sound of bells filled the sky.

Chapter Twenty Two: Christmas Miracle

It was almost impossible to sleep that night. I kept inhaling the scent Santa had left behind. I lay in my bed, eyes wide open. Delia was already snoring. Cory was talking to my father.

As for me, I was lost in my memory of Santa.

I couldn't wrap my head around the fact that I had met him. He was real, he was very much real. I was surprised to learn that he didn't know we existed either. My father said he almost gave Santa a heart attack when he found him.

"We were both shocked," I heard him tell my mother.

By morning, a fresh blanket of snow covered the ground. I hurried out of bed, woke Delia and Cory, and ran to the tree. There, wrapped in beautiful, sparking paper, were our gifts.

"What did you ask Santa for?" my father asked.

He was having breakfast. "Well, go on," he said, motioning toward the tree. "Open your gift."

He and my mother sat as we looked through the many boxes Santa had left us. "I only asked for one gift," Delia said, shaking a box.

"Some of them are from us," my father said.

Delia was first to open hers. "They're beautiful," she said, holding up some dresses.

Cory was next. "I don't think mine will be under the tree," he said.

My father cleared his throat. "I helped Santa with yours."

"You mean, I have my own room now?" Cory asked hopeful.

My father smiled. "I think Sharron is going to be shocked when she wakes up. Her house doubled overnight."

My father looked under the tree. "Now open my gift," he said to Cory.

"You got me a gift?" Cory said, looking under the tree.

He reached under the tree and found a box with his name on it. Cory drew breath when he opened it. "What is it?" Delia asked.

Cory pulled out a beautiful hunting knife, with the words, 'For my son' engraved on it.

My mother kissed my father on the cheek when she saw it. "Now you, Thea," my father said.

I reached for a long box with my name on it.

"That one is from both Santa and me," my father said. "It has magic from both our worlds."

I nodded and began to open my gift. I gasped when I saw a beautiful staff inside the box. It looked like it had been carved right from an oak tree. "What is that?" Delia asked. "Why did Santa give you a stick? What did you ask him for?"

I held up the wooden staff. "I told him I wanted to fly again."

"No more branches," my father said.

Just as I was going to ask if I could go fly it, Sharron walked in looking nervous.

"Oh, no," Cory said. "I think she's going to tell on you."

"What can I do for you, Sharron?" my father asked.

My mother gave her such a look. Sharron looked at her, almost apologizing with her eyes.

"I wouldn't be here if it wasn't important, Emma," Sharron said.

"What is it?" my father asked.

Sharron glanced at me. "It's just that, the humans are talking again."

"And?" my father said.

Sharron looked at my mother. "I'm sorry, Emma."

"What's going on?" my father asked concerned. I noticed he looked my way when he said that.

"Well," Sharron said, eyeing my mother. "The humans are talking about a Christmas miracle."

My father rose to his feet and looked at me. "What kind of miracle?" he asked, his eyes burning through me.

"It turns out," Sharron continued. "Thea's new human friends have family visiting."

"And?" my father said raising his voice.

Sharron swallowed thickly. "Well, the family has a little girl, Abigail is her name. It appears the little girl was deaf."

"Was?" my father said almost slaughtering me with his eyes.

"It would appear," Sharron continued. "When the little girl woke up this morning, she was able to hear."

"Thea!" my father shouted.

I quickly threw paper over myself and tried to make myself invisible.